Freedom Spring

By Kurt M. Vetters

CreateSpace Independent Publishing Platform
North Charleston, South Carolina

First Edition November 2018
Second Edition March 2022

ISBN 978-1-7238161-8-5
Library of Congress Control Number 2018959717

Printed in the United States of America on acid-free paper

Cover layout and design by Joyce Dierschke
Prepress by Bob Allen
Map by Anna Lora Whitley
Interior typography by Hugh Daniel, Author's Corner
Manuscript Preparation by Author's Corner, Raleigh, NC

Cover Photo courtesy National Archives

Published by CreateSpace Independent Publishing Platform, North Charleston, South Carolina

Additional copies may be obtained either by
directly contacting the author:
Kurt Vetters, 317-847-6341 / kvetters@gmail.com

Or by visiting the Author's Corner website:
https://Authors-Corner.net

Or on Amazon.com

To my mother, Sandra Vetters, and to Peggy Towns. Two great Southern women whose passion for family, history and storytelling inspire many.

Contents

Dedication iii
Contents v
Acknowledgements vii
Map viii
Prologue 3
Chapter 1 Time to Go 6
Chapter 2 Found! 10
Chapter 3 The Fort 14
Chapter 4 Rebs! 18
Chapter 5 An Attack 22
Chapter 6 A Truce 26
Chapter 7 The Ruse 29
Chapter 8 Change of Circumstance 35
Chapter 9 The Retreat 39
Chapter 10 A Long Walk 43
Chapter 11 Spies 49
Chapter 12 The Pact 56
Chapter 13 Nashville 59
Chapter 14 Fort Negley 66
Chapter 15 Trust 70
Chapter 16 Assault! 73
Chapter 17 A Good Plan 77
Chapter 18 New Friend 81

Chapter 19 An Exciting Journey.................................... 85
Chapter 20 In the Trenches.. 90
Chapter 21 A New State 94
Chapter 22 The Line 97
Chapter 23 Time to Move..101
Chapter 24 Gators!...104
Chapter 25 Reunion 107
Chapter 26 A Respite..110
Chapter 27 All or Nothing!...113
Chapter 28 Dismissed 118
Chapter 29 Smokey Row 122
Chapter 30 Lucy 126
Epilogue...133
Notes 134
References..135
Study Guide 137
About the Author 150
Also by Kurt M. Vetters, *Confederate Winter*................151

Acknowledgements

Historical novelists are deeply indebted to historians. They put in the work to comb through stacks of dusty documents and microfiche in library corners to pull out the foundations of our stories. Sometimes what emerges is a whole new perspective on the events of history, and history is rewritten as a result. I think this is one such case, and this second edition of Freedom Spring reflects that effort.

The journey started with Peggy Town's terrific book, "Duty Driven." Without her research and scholarship, the story and these characters would not have come to life. She has done so much for her community and her work will affect generations to come.

My old classmate and fellow lineman, Barry Swope, was also instrumental in this book. His knowledge of the Federal right flank at Blakeley and the men who fought there made it come alive for me. We walked the ground many times so he could explain the battle to me.

Lynn Maddox, Tracy Harris and Krista Castillo and the Friends of Fort Negley team also deserve special recognition. They saved the Fort and its surrounding grounds for future generations.

The history of the Battle of Nashville is also little-known but has its own defenders at the Battle of Nashville Trust. Thanks to all who put in the efforts to save that hallowed ground.

I'm indebted to my editors, Nancy Klein and Noelle Steele, and my family of test-readers, especially my wife Donna Steele and my mom, Sandra Vetters. This second edition has been reworked by Donna and Hugh Daniel, my publisher, and it would not be here without them.

Lastly, thanks to my readers, and especially reviewers. You make all the effort worthwhile!

Tennessee
Nashville
Fort Negley
Franklin
N
W
E
S
TENNESSEE RIVER
Jim's Cabin
Athens
Fort Henderson
Atlanta
MISSISSIPPI RIVER
Mississippi
Alabama
Georgia
Vicksburg
Louisiana
White House
New Orleans
Fort Blakeley
Mobile
Pensacola
100 MILES

Freedom Spring

Prologue

The sound of a single gunshot traveled through the warm Alabama air. For Jim Coffee, fourteen years and a lifetime slave to Marse Roberts, that sound was freedom.

Jim walked slowly to the cabin where Marse had lived and raised his family. It had the look of a home at the end of its life. Jim climbed the short, rickety steps to the rough wood of the front porch. Through the open door, he could already see the blood pooling on the floor. He could smell the burnt cordite of Marse's pistol. Marse's hand lay open, fingers gently curled, lifeless, to the sky. Jim sank to his knees on the porch. He did not push the door open to see more. He just watched. Watched the dead hand lie still on the boards.

Jim knew that none of this was good for him. At worst, when Marse was discovered dead, people might jump to the conclusion Jim had murdered him. That meant hanging for sure, and Jim knew he wouldn't get a trial. At best, as soon as it was discovered Marse was dead, he would be taken as a slave to someone else.

One thing he knew with certainty: he knew why Marse had taken his own life.

Marse had shrunk into a bottle over the last year of the war after his wife and daughter succumbed to the fever. News had come yesterday of the death of his son in the great battle around Atlanta, and young Jim had seen Marse's eyes go flat. No. The gunshot was no surprise.

Now, Jim was the only one left.

He and his brother, Jesse – gone this last year, soldiering – had grown up on this little patch of dirt on the side of the mighty Tennessee River, fishing and being hired out to work on the dams and locks that tried to keep the great river in its banks. Their mama was long ago sold down that river to a Louisiana plantation.

He had lived here all his life, but it was not home. It was not his, and with Marse now dead, he imagined this little shack and couple of rickety outbuildings would soon fall into the river, its wood someday floating past his mama.

Jim stood a great long while then slowly backed off the porch. Glancing left, away from the river, he saw the two small, wooden crosses he and Marse had erected for the dead women. He walked in a daze to the workshop, retrieved the shovel, and made his way to the side of Mrs. Robert's grave. He removed his hat, bowed his head. Waited. Nothing. He felt nothing.

The spade bit into the soft earth. Deeper and deeper he dug, careful to line up next to her grave but also more careful not to get too close to its contents. He did not want to uncover her body by accident as he dug Marse's grave.

Complete, he forced himself to the cabin. He steeled himself as he opened the door and brushed at the flies already covering the dead man's face. He pulled the threadbare quilt from the old man's bed and lay it on the ground, away from the pooled and drying blood. Rolling Marse into the blanket was harder than he expected.

At first, Jim tried pulling the body by the shoulders, but the weight of Marse's bloody head kept getting in his way, even wrapped in the quilt. He would have to use the feet. He had no particular love for Marse, but this seemed wrong. It was the lesser of two evils, he decided, and he swung the body around and pulled Marse out of the cabin, thump, thump, thump down the steps, and through the fall leaves to the graveyard. To the hole. And in. Thud.

The quilt came loose from part of Marse's face, and one dead eye looked up from the earth at Jim. Jim sat and tried not to look into the face of the man.

The sun continued to move overhead. The shadows began to lengthen. Finally, Jim mustered his strength and began to fill in the hole. The first shovelful covered Marse's face forever.

When he was done, he did not place a cross at the head of the grave. He simply pushed the shovel into the dirt, handle skyward. It seemed appropriate enough. He turned his back on his old life and walked toward his own cabin.

As Jim entered his tiny room, he looked around. Jesse had carved a little wooden boat for him in happier times, and it lay in one corner, dusty and forgotten. After his brother had run, it was just he and Marse here for almost a year, and no one had been down to see the old man for many months, except with the news his boy was dead. There hadn't been much building since Jesse left, as it was his gift of construction that kept them employed, so they had lived for months on their meager stores and the abundant fish Jim caught. Marse hadn't spoken since Jesse left, and Jim was almost invisible to him – which meant Jim hadn't spoken to anyone in that long, either.

Now, they had all left Jim. Every single person in his life was gone. He was alone. Utterly alone. And the weight of his life crushed him with each breath.

So, Jim just walked. He took nothing. He had no one to say goodbye to, no one to miss him, and as far as he knew, no one to own him anymore. Those people were all gone. He would go east toward the rising sun.

East to find his brother and a new life.

Chapter 1

Time to Go

Jim's world had been very small. Fighting the currents and changing nature of the river kept Jim and Jesse very busy. With every flood came new dams to repair, new ditches to empty, new earth to move. The Indians called this the Singing River, but to Jim and Jesse and the work crews that tried to keep it in its bank, the singing was done by them over pick and shovel.

It was fitting this area once belonged to the Indians. Huge mounds still scattered the landscape that were built by these prior inhabitants. People were always finding arrowheads and tools from these bygone people. There still were some around, but mostly they had been driven out many years before. Jim loved to study the intricacies of their pottery, while Jesse would climb the mounds and marvel at their size and strength.

Jesse was the workhorse of the two. Strong and muscular, Jesse could see the ground in ways most men couldn't. He could channel water down places, away from the bases of buildings, and supervise the work of many older men, always slaves like them. He was talented at building and moving earth. His skill had made a good living for Marse in the old days.

Jim, however, was slighter, more thoughtful and less confident than his older brother. The four years that separated them was magnified by these differences. Jesse respected men who could work hard all day, and Jim could never really keep up.

Jim was also lighter-colored than his brother, who was very dark like their mother. That lightness of color had driven a wedge between the boys as they aged. Not noticing this difference at first, they were inseparable as children, fishing and working and being river slaves for a small family. Their mother, though unquestionably a slave, was also part of the family with Marse and his wife, son and daughter. But as Jim had grown older, things had changed, and even though he did not understand, all the blame seemed to descend on him. Then, when Momma was sold away, Jesse had punched him in the mouth, and the Missus and her children stopped speaking to him. Jim was a sensitive boy, and this rejection for no reason weighed heavily on him.

A year after Momma was sold, the Missus and Rachel died of the fever. And a year after that, Jesse had run off. And now Marse and his son, and only heir, were gone; so, Jim walked.

Slowly at first, Jim stepped away from the shacks by the river. He knew he would not be making these steps back here. He also knew if by chance old Marse Robert's body was discovered before he was gone, there might be hell to pay for him. He had not taken a thing from the house, not even food. One wrong look from someone, almost anyone, and he would be either hanged for murder or sold down river. They would just assume whatever they wanted to believe. Jim knew there was no explaining the actions of white folks.

He walked away from the river. Best to head up where the Yankees were, get past the lines and see if he could start a new life. Thoughts of finding Jesse began to solidify in his head, though he did not know what his welcome would be. Jim had heard many of the local ex-slaves had joined the Yankee army and were manning a fort over toward Athens. He had never been there, but he felt it was toward the rising sun, and his feet pointed him in that direction.

When he reached the big military road, he walked out onto the thoroughfare for just a hundred yards or so, toward the road running north out of Florence. He didn't want to spend much time this close to so many white people, so he planned on turning east from it onto a smaller road as soon as possible. The smaller the roads, the easier to leap into the woods when needed. He had always had the ability to be unseen, to blend with his surroundings, and he prayed that would stand him in good stead on this journey into the unknown.

He heard the clatter of a wagon just in time to jump out of the way. If Jim had a fault, he knew it was daydreaming and getting lost in his own thoughts. He would have to be more careful.

The white man driving the wagon didn't even look at or notice him, but Jim saw a boy about his age, black like him, sitting on the back of the wagon, legs dangling. The boy gazed at Jim. He had seen that boy before. His name was Amos, and he was owned by an old man up the road. Their eyes met, and Jim flipped his thumb up, ever so slightly, and jerked it upward. Amos stared, blinked, then gave a small grin as he faded away. His thumb popped up, too, ever so slightly, in acknowledgement of the secret Jim had just given him.

A less-busy road curved off before him, and he took it, pleased he had gotten off the main road so quickly. Huge trees towered over his head, and it began to get cooler in the shade. He knew it was fast approaching fall, and he knew his months and years, so he reckoned that traveling this time of year in September was as good as any. He should be able to sleep out in the open any night he needed.

He thought about food. Why, oh why, had he not at least brought some fishhooks? At least he could always catch fish. But he wanted nothing from the old place. Nothing but ghosts were there for him now. But fishhooks? How bad could that have been to bring some line and hooks with him?

He heard voices up ahead. He ducked into the brush on the side of the road. He must stop daydreaming! A slave alone, this far away from his place, would bring nothing but trouble. He knew his brother could have talked his way out of a tight spot but not Jim. Too quiet, too afraid.

Two white men walked by him, rifles on their shoulders, talking. Behind them, four black men in chains were led by a rope around the first one's neck. They looked defeated and exhausted in their tattered blue coats as they staggered behind the two armed men. It was hard to tell the color of their trousers, but they looked all the same, almost like they used to be soldiers.

"Right up here's the old military road," one of the white men said. "We're almost done with this sorry lot, but they will bring a handsome reward. I'm going up to Pope's Tavern when we get back and see if they've got any of Nearis Green's sippin' whiskey. Best stuff around."

"I think these negroes will bring even more reward, as they are all four wearing the damned blue coat. These are the first ones I've seen that had signed up for Devil Abe's army," the other man said, then spit a long wad of tobacco juice right next to Jim in the bushes.

As they passed, the last black man looked into the bushes and saw Jim. His eyes widened, and he pursed his lips ever so slightly at him, as if to say, "Shhhhh." And then, they were gone.

Jim didn't breathe for several minutes but lay, terror-stricken, in the brambles. He now knew what was in store for him if he were caught. It could not get worse than that.

Chapter 2

Found!

It took three hard days for Jim to reach Athens. He found the main road outside Florence and always kept it in sight as he traversed it past sleepy little Alabama towns and now to the outskirts of his destination. He had apples and crib corn aplenty, and the water was sweet as it ran down toward the river to his south. Yet, he was hungry for some catfish or squirrel. And salt. What he would give for a little salt right now.

As he emerged from the woods west of Athens, he could see all the way into town. Everything around the city was cleared, and close to him was a big earthen fort in a star shape. The Union flag flew high above it. He could see soldiers in blue all around: marching, camping, cutting wood, just walking. And they were black! Like him!

Jim was naturally a quiet boy; he did not yell with excitement or leap up and run to the men who looked like him. He thought about his next move, grinning all the while. That's when he heard the rustle some thirty feet from him, in the same wood line.

It wasn't much of a rustle. Most folks would think it was a squirrel jumping in the fallen leaves. But Jim knew the sounds of the squirrels. No, this was different. Maybe even a metallic clink within the noise. He could feel the hair on the back of his neck rise. He lay still, so still, barely breathing, and he watched.

As his eyes focused through the scrub, he saw the man. Lying on his belly like Jim, head facing the fort, he looked as if he might be squinting through an eyeglass. Jim had seen these sometimes on the boats at the wharf, but not short like this one appeared to be. The man had a gray cloak and cap. He was bearded and looked rough and weather-beaten. Jim watched the white man watching the fort.

He began to scan the area between himself and the other fellow just to make sure he hadn't missed anything. He was glad he was so dirty and that his skin was the color of coffee because he knew he blended in well with the fall colors of the forest floor. As he moved his eyes left, deeper in the shadows and closer in behind him, he saw a line, almost imperceptible, just a line that should not be there, and then, with horror, the line turned into a cap, the cap turned into a man, and the man was reaching for him. Jim sprang to his feet and sprinted toward the fort as the gloved hand of the new man just swiped at his leg and missed. Jim ran, bursting from the tree line and watching the faces of the dark soldiers stare and then level muskets from all angles at him.

Jim didn't yell. He still hadn't spoken to a soul in months. Even as scared as he was, it was just so foreign for him to make a noise that he ran mute, sprinting as fast as he could toward safety. He waited for the shot to ring out from behind, but none did. He glanced back to the trees: nothing. No movement, no spying eyes, only the empty tree line. It was as if the two men had vanished. Now Jim realized he had a problem.

All these blue-clad men had their rifles pointed at him.

"Get your hands up, young fella," a voice cried. "Are you trying to get yourself plugged?!"

"Rebs, in the trees," Jim said, gasping, his first words bursting forth. "Look!"

Immediately, the closest soldiers in blue jerked their rifles toward the woods, past Jim. They began to spread out and walk slowly toward the trees, but the man who first spoke to Jim kept his rifle trained on him. Even though he had a trusting face, he did not seem to be totally trusting of Jim, not just yet.

"Who are you?" the man said. "And what were you doing in those trees? Are you a Rebel spy we done caught?"

"No, I'm just Jim."

"Nothing here, Sarge," came the cry back from the woods, and the eyebrows raised as they looked at Jim.

"Nothing in there but you, young fellow, say my boys. What say you to that?" the sergeant said. Jim noticed the three stripes on the man's arms, different from most of the others.

I'll show you where he lay, Jim wanted to say, but the words were hard for him, speechless for so long. He looked up at the man, pleading and fear in his eyes; he just held his palms apart, arms out. He had traveled so far, hidden for so long, and now that he thought he was in safety's arms, he was alone again. His shoulders slumped.

"Jim? Is that you, little brother?"

The voice sounded so familiar, then there he was: Jesse – tall, strong, stripes on his arms, too, and carrying a cane stick, not a rifle.

The other sergeant's eyes darted to Jesse, then back to Jim, and he lowered his rifle.

"Jesse!" Jim cried and ran to his brother. Jesse caught him by the top of the head and held him at arm's length a moment, looked him in the face, stopping him before they could embrace. He leaned down, examined him, turned his head one way, then the other.

"What are you doing here, little brother?" Jesse sneered, catching Jim off guard. He looked up at his brother in wonder and confusion. "You run off from your daddy? Does the old man know you're here?"

"Geez, Sergeant Coffee," the other sergeant said, "go easy on the kid. He looks like hell."

"You shut the hell up, Cowley," Jesse growled, then pulled his brother to him, not so much in an embrace but in a painful squeeze, crushing him against him. Turning, he brought Jim under his arm but not out of his steel grip.

"Walk those woods, Cowley. I want to know if there is anything in there. Tracks, any sign we are being watched. Rumors are all around that Forrest is on the march. We need to know if he is headed this way, and for God's sake, move your pickets out at least to these woods. It’s a pretty sad state when my idiot brother can sneak up on our whole garrison!”

Chapter 3

The Fort

Jesse took Jim into the fort, Fort Henderson he called it, and they climbed a wooden watchtower. Jesse told the two guards in the tower to leave, and he pulled out a big piece of salt pork from his haversack and handed it to Jim as they leaned on the walls, overlooking the surrounding countryside.

"Well, little brother, spit it out." Jesse said. "How did you end up running toward our fort today?"

Jim quietly devoured the pork, savoring the salt in his mouth. He thought about what Jesse had said: "your Daddy." Jim didn't have a father. He knew that. He had almost been in the grasp of a confederate soldier ten minutes ago, but all he could think about were the words Jesse had said.

"My daddy?" Jim finally said.

"Of course, yo' daddy!" Jesse erupted. "Don't tell me you never knew Marse was your daddy? Why do you think Mama got sold down the river 'bout the time we could start to tell you looked like a colored version of him?"

Jim leaned forward and stared at his brother as these words washed over him.

"You really didn't ever figure that out, did you boy?" Jesse tossed his head back and laughed. "You poor ignorant child. You must have mush for brains!"

Jim let the pork drop to the ground. His mouth hung open, tears welling in his eyes. He had never considered in all his years that Marse was his father. It had never occurred to him. And now, after all he had just been through, to hear this as his greeting.

Tears, pain, realization of so much coursed through him, over him. His soul hurt. He was even more a no-one than he had been moments before. He was an "other."

Jesse softened. Not much, but he knew pain when he saw it, and he felt sorry for this poor child suffering before him. Yet, sympathy was not his way, not when he had built and run this fort. He could not let this whining kid, even if he was his own flesh and blood, undermine all he had built.

"Ok, now, straighten up." Jesse said, silencing the boy. "Start at the beginning. How did you come here? Tell me what you have seen and anything I need to know. I have men's lives here that depend on me."

Jim wiped his tears, stood a little straighter, and told Jesse about the death of Marse's son at Atlanta, about Marse's suicide, and about walking away. He told him about seeing the four colored soldiers, captured, with the chains around their necks, and he told him about the two Confederate soldiers in the woods, spying on them.

"You have to believe me, Jesse, about those two men in the woods. They were like ghosts, but they were there, honest," Jim pleaded.

"Oh, I believe you, Jim," Jesse said. "Those were Forrest's scouts, and we have had a feeling they were watching us for some time. Our officers haven't been too concerned, however." He gestured to several white men in blue coats and tall boots lounging under a shade tree left inside the fort, playing cards and smoking.

"What do you mean 'your' fort?" Jim asked his brother.

"Those white officers are in command here, but they pretty much tell me what they want done, and I tell the rest of the soldiers. They all look to me as the builder of this fort. It's just like building back at home, except here I do it as a free man; well, as free as any man can be in the Army." Jesse said. "But they pay us, or at least they say they will when the payroll wagon comes in."

"Our job here is to guard this town, which you see over there, and this railroad line between the town and us. We have scouts and a small garrison of soldiers up there in the town. They are always on the watch for rebel spies and saboteurs. If a cavalry raid by one of General Forrest's columns rides in, we barricade ourselves in the fort and make it hot for them. They ride off without much damage to either side."

"How long have you been here, Jesse?" Jim asked. "I missed you," he finished in a small voice.

Jesse clenched his jaw, brow furrowed, so much pain wrapped in those last words.

"Every time I looked at you, I saw the reason for Mama being gone. Rachel and the Missus were the same. Nobody could talk about it, but nobody could be around you and not know what was going on. It wasn't a big deal when you were little, but as you grew, ooooh boy, we all knew. I guess everybody but you.

"Well, anyway, I ran. I made my way by night up to Pulaski and signed up for the army. I'm now the sergeant major of the 110th United States Colored Infantry. And I run this show. Plus, when the officers found out I knew how to build, they assigned me to build this fort. Oh, we had white engineers who laid out where the cannon needed to go, how the trenches needed to be laid out and such, but the building of the fort and everything else, they left to us. I've been too busy to think about nurse-maiding you."

Jesse's complexion, already dark, darkened even more.

"After April last year and the massacre of the colored troops at Ft. Pillow by Forrest's men, we had to make this place stronger than ever. Word is this is the strongest Union fort outside of Nashville, and I'm damn proud of it. We can defend this post for weeks. We have our own well and plenty of ammunition, and we know how to use it."

"What happened at Ft. Pillow, Jesse?" Jim asked. "I've never heard of that. The Marse didn't speak to me for a whole year."

"Crazy old man," Jesse said. "Well, over by Memphis, a fort like this one was attacked by Forrest. The garrison was all colored soldiers. They fought like hell but were overrun. Lots of the colored soldiers killed. Now, they knew they would go back to slavery if captured, but to be killed after surrendering?" Jesse paused. "We know our fate if we lose a fight here."

Jesse's voice trailed off as he scanned the horizon. He stopped, looking toward the east and town.

"Jim, what do you see there?!"

Jim looked and could see blue troops scurrying out of the town of Athens, heading for the fort. Before he could say anything, Jesse, no longer an older brother but a leader, started yelling orders.

Jim watched as his brother slid down the ladder followed by two guards who scurried back up. Jim stayed and had a ringside view of all the goings-on. He was scared, but he also was hungry. He picked up the salt pork from the floor and began to eat.

Chapter 4

Rebs!

A train rolled up the rail line into Athens from the south, and Jim watched as more blue-clad soldiers, several with red-soaked bandages covering arms and heads and faces, piled out of it. These soldiers joined the others rushing toward the safety of the fort.

"What's yer name, boy?" one of the pair of sentries that had just joined Jim in the tower asked. "And are you really Sergeant Major Coffee's brother?"

"Jim, and yes, I am."

"I'm Adler. This here's my friend, Lucius. You keep your head down, but you're as safe up here as can be. You can watch with us all the commotion until things get hot. But I will tell you," he looked pointedly at Jim, "you do as we say, lickety-split."

They all watched as the white officers scattered to their posts, saw that the black soldiers were already in their positions long before they arrived. The ramparts were manned and bristling with bayonets.

Ft. Henderson was a big earthen fort, Jim saw, with five sharp corners jutting out from the sides. Two cannons were placed at intervals, facing south away from town. A deep ditch surrounded the whole place except for an opening gate facing the town. All around the fort were sharp stakes and brush facing outward. Inside the fort were ramparts the soldiers stood on, with logs across the top under which they could fire and protect their heads.

"Those are called head-logs," Adler said, noticing Jim looking around the fort. "Nobody wants to get hit in the face or head, so we put the thickest logs we can find up on top and hope the Minnie balls hit them and not us."

Jim saw the United States flag on a tall pole in the middle of the fort, surrounded by low-slung earthen-walled huts with wooden roofs covered by more dirt.

"That's where the white officers stay, so if it gets hot, you skedaddle over there. We'll let your brother know where to find you. There's a last-ditch trench line around that area, and it's the safest spot in the camp.

"Do not run over there," Adler added, pointing to the northern side of the fort. Jim noticed a big hole going underground into what looked like a covered room. "That's the powder magazine. If that blows, it will blow half the fort up. We keep the ammunition for the rifles and cannon in there. Big boom!"

Jim nodded. They saw more commotion to the southwest, generally in the area that Jim had just come from and where he had seen the two Confederate soldiers in the woods. The pickets that had gone through the woods looking for these men came hustling back through the trees. For the first time, the whole garrison heard shots fired in anger. The battle was approaching!

Adler and Lucius looked at each other, wide-eyed.

"Finally, we get to fight them Rebs!" Lucian cried. The men all over the fort began to yell and holler, waving their caps in the air and standing up to see what was happening.

"Get down, you sons of whores!" Jim could hear his brother yelling. Other black soldiers with stripes on their arms were doing the same thing. A knot of white officers began to gather at the top of the southwest rampart.

The soldiers began to crouch again. A white officer on a horse rode through the gate and trotted out southwest to meet the troops coming back in. They stayed in a loose line, Jim saw, and crouched just inside the wood line, firing. He watched a messenger from the officers run to Jesse, who pulled about a hundred men out of the defenses on the north side and sent them marching with another sergeant out of the fort to join the men firing from the fort toward the Rebels.

The men from the train staggered in, bloodied and exhausted. Jim watched their leader, a tall, thin white officer with a bandage on his arm, salute a man in a tall black hat.

"That's the colonel, our commander," Adler said, not so much to Jim but more to hide his own nervousness. "Colonel Wallace Campbell. He cuts a fine figure with that big hat, don't he?"

Jim noticed a saddled horse near him and a young boy in a blue coat holding the reins. Other horses were being saddled and brought to the same spot.

The wind began to change as the firefight intensified to the southwest. Jim was in barely rags, and he shivered in the tower. Adler noticed. He yelled to a soldier below.

"Joshua, go get my coat out of the tent, and grab one for Sergeant Coffee's brother, too."

The man named Joshua looked to his corporal, two stripes on his sleeve, who motioned for him to go, and he took off at a run. He was back in less than a minute with three blue overcoats for the men in the exposed tower.

Jim felt the coarse wool of the coat slide over his hands as he slipped it on. The feeling of putting on that coat was thrilling. He did not feel so alone now that he was wearing the same color of his people. His people, manning the fort on this cool Alabama night. Adler noticed that, too.

"Feels mighty good to be wearing the blue, don't it, Jim? He smiled at the boy. "It must have been hell growing up with that brother of yours. He's smart, but he is a hard man."

Men now began streaming from all sides of the fort back toward the gate. The white officer turned his stallion and galloped back to the knot of officers. His words were lost in the wind, but he gestured wildly with his sword, and Jim saw the colonel nod. The mounted officer rode back to the trees, shouted some orders, and the picket line began to move slowly back to the fort and then filed in, each taking his place on the ramparts as directed.

Even the soldiers out by the railroad line began filing in. Just a few out toward Athens seemed all that were left as darkness began to fall. The sun slid behind the trees to the southwest, the same trees Jim had hidden in earlier. The whole fort gasped as one, as rebel horsemen began to appear at its edge. They sat on their mounts, just out of rifle range, and watched.

Then came the cannon, crashing through the woods and lining up, aimed at the fort. Just a few, but they looked dark and foreboding. The knot of officers jumped down from the top of the redoubt and peered under the head log.

Jim could feel the tension building as nine-hundred men held their breath.

Chapter 5

An Attack

Lucian and Adler spoke quietly to one another, and then Adler said, "Jim, you best get down from here now. Our relief is coming up shortly, and if your brother knows we let you stay up here exposed in this fight, he will have our hides. You see that boy holding the colonel's horse? He's about your age, and he has a good bunk right beside the colonel's quarters. Tell him who you are and that we told you to go stay in his bunk till this is all over. We will see you after. Then we want to hear some stories about your brother!"

Jim swept his eyes around the fort one last time before climbing down. He could see his brother with his soldiers on the south wall and knew he would be in the thick of the fight. He was proud of his brother and wished Jesse could see him in his blue coat. It dwarfed him, of course, but he was proud of it, nonetheless.

The first shots erupted from the rebel cannon as his feet hit the ground. No noise in his life was as loud as the boom of those cannons firing as one at the fort. The whistle of the shells arcing toward them, the scream of the air broken by the shells, and then four deafening explosions right over the fort. Death roared over their heads, flames spewing small pieces of flesh-ripping iron across the encampment.

As Jim ran toward the horses, he could see little deadly puffs of red dirt jump up all around, and he could also hear the screams of men falling with wounds to their backs as the shell fragments ripped into them from behind. The ramparts were solid, but they were not ready for this arcing carnage from behind, from inside the fort!

Jim made it to the colonel's orderly just in time before the next four shots fired into the fort. The young soldier was doing everything he could to hold the horse steady as it reared and bucked to the noise and disaster inside. He grabbed the reins with the young man to help steady the horse; their eyes locked for an instant. Then, a piece of exploding shell ripped through the boy's chest. He fell, gasping, then lay still, leaving Jim to hold the colonel's horse alone. The boy's blood pumped over Jim's shoeless feet. And still the shells came. Jim held the horse for all he was worth.

Hours passed and the shelling continued, every shot a direct hit on the fort. The horse bit at Jim, eyes rolling in its head as it pulled and kicked and yanked at the rope with every shell burst, but Jim held him.

Jim's arms were soon exhausted and sweat poured into his eyes. He gripped the rope in his teeth and wrapped it under his arm, trying to free a hand to reach the dead boy's cap laying close on the ground.

His bloody feet became so cold, he realized he needed something to keep them warm. He looked at the shoes of the dead boy, and tears welled in his eyes. He must have them, though. Holding the reins in his teeth again, he crouched down and stole the boy's shoes. He felt like a ghoul.

Fires roared everywhere. A blockhouse toward Athens burned and backlit the fort so the rebel gunners could not miss. All night long, Union soldiers streamed into the fort from their far-flung posts. Rumor passed around they had even seen General Forrest himself, dining in Athens. This was no raid; this was a full-scale assault by the most feared general in the Confederate army!

No one slept that night in Ft. Henderson. The dead and dying lay everywhere, illuminated by phantom flashes as the shells exploded. Just before dawn, with just the hint of light in the eastern sky, it seemed all hell broke loose again. The shots came doubly quick, and the casualties continued to mount. Jim prayed for his brother's safety but also for his own sanity. All he knew to do was hold the colonel's horse and hope he did not die.

Then, light. The sun broke the horizon, and the firing stopped. That was a blessing, but the carnage that could now be seen in the strengthening light of day was sickening. Ripped and torn bodies littered the inside of the fort. Every structure inside that could burn was burned or burning. But not the magazine, thank goodness. Jim could not see his brother anywhere.

A gray-clad rider approached the fort. Jim could not see the flag of truce from where he stood in the entrenchments, but he heard the call to hold fire go all around the fort. He was right behind the colonel on the rampart, so he could see him unsteadily mount the wall and listen to the Confederate entreaty to surrender. He could not hear it all, but he did hear the last part about the colored soldiers going back into slavery. The fort erupted in boos and yells of "No surrender" from the black troops. Colonel Campbell looked around at his depleted, yet still fight-worthy garrison, and refused the offer.

So, the cannonade began again. Now the horror which had been so hidden by darkness, was in full view in its macabre dance of death. Each explosion brought death, and more and more men huddled and tried to bury themselves in the earth. They dug holes in the embankments, pulled head logs off to cover their holes, and anything they could to shield themselves from the fierce bombardment. Two more hours of death from the air were endured before the next pause. The silence was deafening. After so many hours of bombardment, it was almost more frightening.

With the pause, another flag of truce from a gray rider.

The colonel, now slightly bleeding from his ear, mounted the rampart and listened again to Forrest's entreaty: "Surrender to stop this useless effusion of blood, or it will be on your head when the assault leads to massacre." The troops inside once again yelled their defiance, but this time the colonel paused. The rebel officer, out of sight but not out of earshot, asked the Union colonel to ride outside the works and see the strength of his foe. He agreed.

As the colonel climbed down from the works, he ordered his

horse and one other brought up, and he motioned for Jim to come forward. Jim stared in disbelief, but just as the colonel was too exhausted to realize that Jim was not his regular servant, neither did Jim have the energy or forethought to do anything except lead the skittish horse to its master.

"Boy, I'm tired, and this horse is crazed. You will lead it out with me as we see the enemy camp," the colonel said to Jim. He mounted, followed by another officer on horseback. Jim led the horse out the gate and into the heart of the enemy.

Chapter 6

A Truce

Compared to the carnage inside the fort, outside seemed almost peaceful. No shells were coming from inside the fort, as they were saving their ammunition for the expected assault. Jim walked the colonel's horse and saw no dead or wounded Confederates. When they entered the wood line, he could smell the cordite and gunpowder that hung in the air, and he could see the cannon and their crews watching him with scowls. He knew they did not like to see black men in uniform, even boys.

Jim looked, wide-eyed, at everything. He had an eye for detail, and it was fascinating for him to see the difference in these soldiers compared to the Union troops in the fort. They were rough-looking men; beards, every sort of uniform imaginable, and they looked like they grimly knew their jobs well. He could see patches in the wheels of some of the cannons; it looked like they had used whatever wood was at their disposal. One cannon spoke was raw wood, unpainted, and it stood out against the others. It looked like it had been freshly repaired. But it also looked strong enough to hold up to a bombardment of hours into Ft. Henderson.

Jim followed the rebel courier with the flag of truce, until they stopped just inside the rebel lines. It was still wooded here, but through the trees, he saw a group of uniformed riders approaching, all gray and dusty.

Fierce.

That was the only word Jim could think of when the rebel general rode up to his poor, battered, exhausted colonel. His red-lined cape flashed, and the two pistols at his belt looked menacing. But his eyes. His eyes were like two bright fires directed right at them. Jim imagined they had the same intensity as the moment fire belched from a cannon's mouth.

"Suh, I am General Nathan Bedford Forrest, and I aim to see you surrendered today or overrun. It is simply your choice. You and your men have only had a taste of what my army can offer, and you have done your duty in defending your post, but now I bring to bear too many guns, too many men, too much force for your small garrison."

Forrest spoke politely, but his words had great import.

"I shall make sure your white officers are exchanged for prisoners of equal rank among our own army, and I will grant them parole today. I will return your colored soldiers to their rightful place with their masters and make sure they are treated well. I have no desire to see so many killed today," Forrest said.

Colonel Campbell hesitated, looking left and right to see what number of troops was visible.

"Why don't we take a ride around the lines, Colonel, so you can see what you're up against?"

At that moment, another Confederate officer rode up, and Jim could see his dusty column of men arriving in the distance.

"Welcome, General Wheeler," Forrest said quickly before the other man could speak.

Jim noticed a slight hesitation from the man, and then he saw a spark of recognition on the new officer's face, like he understood a secret message.

"Thank you, General Forrest, I've brought all seven-thousand of my men to this fight today. When do we begin the assault?"

Forrest turned to Colonel Campbell, a look of victory in his eyes. "Let us ride the lines, Colonel, so you can see what we can bring to bear."

They followed Forrest and his entourage at a walk, slowly circling the fort. The colonel was not an accomplished rider, and the poor horse was still completely spooked, but Jim held the reins and guided them through the rebel camps. It was an awesome display of power, with grimy, gritty, gray cavalrymen on all sides, and more and more cannons were seen in every new woodlot. They passed by the town and the burnt-out blockhouse, and Jim noticed something.

That same cannon with the repaired wheel stood in front of him again. The same one they had seen on the west side of the fort. That was odd, and Jim looked at the colonel and his aide to see if they noticed.

Now, Jim was really watching, and he started to see the same men he had seen earlier, just now they were on this side of the fort, not the other. As they moved around to the southern side of the fort, Jim looked behind him and saw, just barely, that the men they passed were collecting their gear and getting ready to move. The soldiers had that look that all slaves knew well, watching for that moment when the master was out of sight.

On the southwest side, Jim saw that same cannon again, but this time, the gunners were leaning around it, hiding it as best they could. It was like they sensed it might give the game up. They seemed to look closely at the colonel and his aide, but no one really watched Jim at all. As usual in his life, he was mostly invisible. And his face would never let on that he knew anything, anyway, one of the skills of the enslaved.

When they arrived back at the road into the fort, Forrest turned again to the colonel.

"As you can see, Suh, you are defeated by weight of numbers alone. Please do not sacrifice the lives of so many men today when you have done your duty. You have delayed us on our raid, and you will be honored by your people for that. But you face the weight of both General Wheeler and me, and you stand no chance," Forrest said.

The colonel, already pale and now sickly looking, looked around once more, and managed a feeble nod.

Jim swallowed hard but said nothing.

Chapter 7

The Ruse

Jim was faced with a dilemma as he walked the colonel back to the fort. He knew they had been tricked, that the Rebels had moved the same men and cannon around the fort to make it look like they were stronger than they were. Jim had never been in a battle before, though, and he certainly was not going to bring his discovery up to the colonel, but he couldn't wait to get to the fort to tell his brother. He would know what to do!

The huge gates opened, and Jim saw every face in the garrison staring at them. He felt tiny amidst all these men. He began to doubt himself. Had he made a mistake? Were they really playing a trick on them? Jim was not a boy of many words, but he knew his words held very powerful implications for the Union soldiers.

His brother approached, not looking at him at all, just with eyes on the colonel. Jim noticed he held back. Their party stopped inside the gate, and all the other white officers came running. Jim could see that his brother, though clearly important to the defense of Ft. Henderson, was not part of this group.

The colonel dismounted heavily, and Jim stood there, reins in hands, feeling overwhelmed. Jesse walked to him and, without taking his eyes off the colonel, asked "What did you see out there, Tom?"

"No, Jesse, it's me," Jim whispered, barely getting the words out.

Jesse swept his gaze quickly to him, startled, then angry, to land on a familiar face. "What the hell were you doing out there, you idiot?!" he hissed under his breath.

Jim froze. What had he done? Had he made some grave error?

Jesse snatched the reins and led Jim and the horse away from the gathering knot of white officers. When they were safely out of earshot, he turned on Jim, horse between them and the small command group. He put his face right down into Jim's.

"So, again, what the hell were you doing?" Jesse's spittle hit Jim's face.

Jim's eyes widened. His mind rushed in a million directions. "I…I… led the horse."

"Well, I see that, you little imbecile. How did that happen?"

"Tom was… was… killed, if that was his name. I only just met him, and a cannon fragment killed him. So, I held the horse last night. Did I do something bad?" he asked, eyes downcast.

Jesse did not soften. "You could have gotten the colonel killed or worse. You don't know what you're doing, and I told you to stay out of trouble. And where'd you get that coat? You're not a soldier, you're just a boy!"

Jim mustered every ounce of courage he had to tell Jesse what he knew, and he tried more than once to get the words out. He stammered "I… I… they… they… are tricking…"

He never finished. The colonel's voice, shattered in a way Jim had never thought possible from someone of his authority, came to them from around the horse.

"We are surrendered."

Jesse whirled away from Jim to catch the news. He could hear the order rippling down the ranks of blue-clad soldiers, and the groan inside the fort turned to wailing. All the black soldiers knew what this meant for them. Back to bondage, back to the bite of the whip. Their lot would be so much worse for serving the Yankees.

Jesse turned back to Jim in a flash, truly angry now but also dumbstruck. "What did you say? Tricked? How?"

"They moved their men and cannons around, so that they looked like there were more of them than they are," Jim stammered. He had gotten the words out, but they were too late.

"How do you know this?" Jesse scoffed. Jim told him about the cannon with the repaired spoke. It took time to get the words out. He knew he was not convincing, but he knew he had to let Jesse know.

By then, soldiers were coming down from the ramparts and stacking their rifles into little pyramids all around the fort. Jesse looked one last time at Jim, searching his face for the truth, the veracity of this horrible news, mingled with the shock of the change so quickly in their fortune. At last, he believed Jim was telling the truth, at least the truth he knew, just being a boy.

"You better be right," he spat as he turned and walked toward the colonel.

Jim saw him approach, salute and exchange a few words. The colonel tossed his hand dismissively in the air and looked over at Jim. It was too late. And he was just a boy, so no one would really believe, nor care, about what he knew or thought he knew.

Jim watched Jesse's shoulders go limp, his proud bearing gone almost immediately. The colonel did not look at Jesse again. He turned away, and Jim could see the wall between black and white rise up, rise up and overwhelm them both. They were, in that instant, no longer colonel and sergeant major but white man and black man. Jim knew Jesse knew it, too.

The wailing in the fort was turning to resigned depression. Jim saw it in every man's face. Except the white officers. They seemed...relieved. It was like the stress of the last twenty-four hours had suddenly vanished. Jim hadn't moved with the horse. He really didn't know what to do. But he stood close to the Union officers as they gathered together and could make out snippets of their conversation.

What he heard frightened him.

"At least we won't have to fight with these damn darkies any longer," one said. The reply was chilling.

"If we had, Forrest would have had us hanged. At least under these terms, we will be paroled and home in a few days. And these damn men will be back in chains where they belong."

Jim had hoped these white men would be different. He hoped the blue uniform changed everything, but now, he knew, it did not change men inside.

One officer seemed different, however. His voice was not as brash as the others, more reasoned, "This is a terrible thing, gentlemen. We promised these soldiers something more than this. We promised them freedom, and they did everything and more that we asked of them."

"Lieutenant Green, you are one surefire idealist. Didn't you say you want to come down here after the war and start a school? Pshah! We all have known you believe these slaves can be good soldiers, but they are not like us. I, for one, got a promotion to take this position, and it got me out of being cannon fodder in the lines. I never thought for one minute we could fight with these," he hesitated, "men."

Lieutenant Green walked by Jim, paused, put his hand on his shoulder just briefly, a human acknowledgement, and walked past toward the parade ground where the colored troops were milling around the flagpole. Jim watched the flag … bright red, white and blue, but now smoke-stained and tattered, slowly begin to lower. Jim saw Jesse wade into the middle of the throng and start to bark orders.

"I'll be damned if we are going to walk out of here with our heads down. No sir. Form up! Form up! Stop that flag." Jesse roared. The men began to form into their companies and straighten their backs, chins up just a bit.

Lieutenant Green took his place at the head of the formation, saluted Jesse, standing at ramrod attention, and the bugler began to play the mournful notes of Taps, not Retreat, as usual. The sound didn't mean anything to Jim, but he could see the effect on the soldiers as each note played. Tears streamed down all their faces as the flag slowly lowered. Two soldiers stepped forward. They grasped the flag and stretched it between them. With each somber, triangular fold, Jim could see the men's shoulders sag. Both were openly weeping.

Jim looked at his brother. He could see the pain in his eyes. He imagined the feeling that must be coursing through him. To have his position, the assurance of victory, the obvious pride Jesse felt in being part of the Union army, now gone.

The colonel walked forward to take possession of the colors. He turned to the massed formation.

"Soldiers, you have done your duty, and your nation is proud of you. This will be a hard road ahead, but it is within you to stay the course, accept your treatment and know that we will win this war, and soon, you will be free men again. It has been an honor serving as your commander." Colonel Campbell saluted, turned on his heel with the carefully folded flag and walked toward Jim.

When the colonel reached Jim, without even a look, he mounted his horse and said, "You are to stay with me, boy. We are to be paroled, and you're my servant, so follow the horse. No one will bother you, but do not look back."

All the white officers mounted and slowly walked their horses out of the gate. Jim looked out of the corner of his eye to see Lieutenant Green talking to Jesse and slipping a scrap of paper to him before he, too, mounted and followed the colonel. Jesse stared at his brother, eyes wide, watching him leave. All the now-surrendered soldiers watched their white officers abandon them. At the gate, General Forrest and his staff accepted the swords of the Union officers.

As the small ceremony concluded, gray-clad soldiers rushed into the fort and began yelling and screaming at the colored soldiers. A few of the Confederate officers rode into the fort, swords drawn, but they appeared nonchalant as the abuse started. Jim could see the colored troops being knocked about, caps knocked off heads. He heard orders shouted to turn their coats inside out. Within seconds, dust covered the whole parade ground, and only shouted curses could be heard.

Jim followed the colonel and the other officers out, away from Jesse, away toward the north.

Chapter 8

Change of Circumstance

One moment, Jesse was the sergeant major of a Union Army regiment, and within seconds of the flag lowering, he was a slave again. At least in the eyes of the Southern soldiers pouring through the gates of the fort. The abandoned soldiers had all heard of the massacre at Ft. Pillow, and were expecting to be slaughtered, but there were enough rebel officers riding amongst the men, flashing the flats of their swords, to keep the wild Confederate soldiers at bay. It was humiliation they were after, not death.

Orders were shouted first to strip off their boots. Oh, these fine Union Army boots, the best footwear any of them had ever owned! When a man owned only the clothes on his back, to lose those precious shoes was terrible. Jesse noticed quickly, though, that the footwear of the Confederates was in shambles, and the rebel soldiers were searching quickly for boots that fit them. After that, the Union soldiers started flinging their shoes in opposite directions, just to make it hard to match pairs, a small but meaningful gesture to them.

While they were ordered to turn their coats inside out, the sergeants had their stripes ripped from their sleeves as they did so. The Union soldiers knew who their leaders, even without the stripes sewn on their arms, but the Confederates would acknowledge no rank among these ex-slaves, and they were making sure the colored troops knew it.

Jesse still held the roughly folded note secretly slipped to him from Lieutenant Green in his hand and quickly pushed it into his pants pocket. He had not seen its contents yet, but he knew Lieutenant Green had always been a friend to the men, and he knew that whatever it said must be important.

Jesse studied the situation and looked for opportunities. Having been responsible for these 900 men for so long had made his wits sharp. He noticed one thing right away. There were not as many of these rebel soldiers as they had expected. They were certainly abusing and pushing and shoving his men around, as fearless as anyone would expect General Forrest's men to be, but their numbers did not actually seem to be any larger than the Union men in the fort.

Jesse realized his brother had been correct. They had fallen prey to one of Forrest's famous ruses. It was the most humiliating blow of them all. Their white officers had surrendered them to a lesser foe, and that was hard to bear.

As the humiliation and thievery slowly died down, the Confederate officers began to take control. Jesse saw General Forrest for the first time, and he immediately understood his fearsome reputation. Jesse started barking orders to his men and was immediately struck down with a blow from a sword to the top of his head. Just the flat of the sword, but it was a blow strong enough to fell even a man like him.

"There is no more rank among you." General Forrest bellowed. "Your days in the Union Army are over. Now, I must place you back into servitude. It will be hard, but you will survive." After such an assault on the Union soldiers, Jesse was surprised at the almost gentle nature of Forrest's words. "We have all had a hard road these last years. My men and I," he gestured toward his own men, now encircling the colored soldiers, "have also had a difficult road. We are the fighters, we understand deprivation. We understand pain and loss, and we know you feel loss now, too. We understand because we have seen battle, and now, you have also. Yes, we have stripped you of some dignity today. And yes, we have placed you back into servitude. But we know you were prepared for battle, and we do respect that.

"But, let me warn you," Forrest continued. "we are the exception. While you are under our guard, we will endeavor to treat you well. We expect the same treatment. Follow our orders, and you will be fine. But as you move to your new home, do not let them know you were Union soldiers. In the rear, to men not accustomed to battle, they will have deeper prejudice. Do not let them know you were former Union soldiers, or it could go very badly for you."

Jesse looked around him at his former subordinates and watched these words sink in. The men were starting to shuffle uncomfortably. Many were taking off their Union caps, their proud Union caps, the few that had not been knocked off, and were gently placing them on the ground. They were starting to listen to Forrest, and Jesse could feel his control over them slipping away. He was not the big man anymore, and he knew it. Forrest was the genius he had always heard, and in just a few seconds, he had become the slave-owner these men had known, doling out encouragement but always with the threat of dark violence behind it.

"You will be starting a long march south to the fortifications of Mobile. The walk will take weeks, but you will find yourself in warmer climes soon. As you march and camp, dye your uniforms to take the blue away. You do not want to present yourselves as former Union soldiers. Strip away your military bearing and become your old selves. I pray you do this for your safety. Godspeed you on your journey, and I pray you survive this terrible war."

Forrest wheeled his horse, saluted a subordinate and trotted back just a few paces. His performance was complete. Jesse knew in an instant he had turned these Union soldiers into slaves with just a few words, and he had done it masterfully.

From his vantage point close to General Forrest, he heard the man speak to another officer.

"Excellent work, Colonel Wheeler." Forrest said to the other man. "When you rode up with your small command, and we were discussing surrender with the Yankee colonel, you caught on quickly when I called you 'General Wheeler.' We saw his eyes widen when he thought your command of two hundred was actually seven thousand under General Joseph Wheeler. An excellent accident in names that had substantial consequences for us this day."

Jesse watched all the officers around General Forrest laugh. His shoulders sagged as the truth of Jim's words rang even truer. If only he had believed his brother more quickly, he might have been able to stop all this. The blame of the entire surrender now fell heavily on Jesse, and his depression grew.

It deepened as they were herded out of the fort, just a mob of downcast and humiliated slaves. They all realized as they passed the gate that they outnumbered their captors. But they were now unarmed in spirit as well as arms. They all knew they had a long walk ahead, that they were headed to the deep south, farther and farther away from the freedom they had briefly tasted.

Chapter 9

The Retreat

Jim followed the swordless Union officers for ten miles before anyone even noticed him.

"Tom, did you bring my camp gear?" Colonel Campbell asked in his direction, finally turning in his saddle.

Jim stared at him, dumbfounded.

"What?! Who are you?!" the colonel roared.

"I'm Jim," Jim stuttered. "Tom was killed in one of the first blasts." Jim, as always not used to saying much, was taken aback that he even got these words out.

The colonel was so angry, veins stood out all over his neck and face. He wheeled on Jim, knocking him to the ground, all the while groping for his nonexistent sword. Luckily for Jim, Lieutenant Green intervened, riding up to the colonel and grabbing his reins as Jim cowered in the dirt.

"Sir, sir, he's just a boy. I believe he is Sergeant Major Coffee's little brother, just come into camp yesterday. Is that right, boy?" Lieutenant Green asked Jim, still trying to diffuse the situation. Jim had seen this before: when a white man had things go wrong, it was easy to find a black boy to take out his frustration on.

"Yessir," Jim said. "Just got here yesterday. I walked the colonel's horse all around the field yesterday after Tom was killed. I guess we just looked alike, and I was holding the colonel's horse when Tom got hit." Jim could feel the words coming a little easier now. He had spoken more in the last two days than he had in a year, and his tongue was coming back to him.

The colonel's gaze pierced into Jim. The focus of all his wrath, his frustration, his anger boiled out at Jim through those eyes.

"Shoot him." The colonel said, turning back north and dismissing him out of hand as he rode away.

Jim's head dropped. His life would end here on this dusty road.

To his surprise, Lieutenant Green jumped down from his horse and helped him up. "Don't worry, Jim," he whispered. "He doesn't mean it. It's been a hard day for him. You just stay back, and we will be up to the Union lines in a mile or two. I will introduce you to one of the other colored regiments, and you can sign in and join. I bet you'll be like your brother, an excellent soldier. Stay back a ways, and when we get to the lines, you follow me."

"Thank you, sir," Jim said. This unexpected kindness surprised Jim.

Just as Lieutenant Green had predicted, within a mile, they came to a trestle bridge with a big blockhouse guarded by both white and black Union troops. Everyone was in a high state of alert, and soldiers were hurrying everything to the north side of the bridge as fast as they could.

Jim watched and listened as Colonel Campbell relayed the news to the Union commander at this small station. It was obvious they were planning on leaving quickly, and this news about the surrender of Ft. Henderson sped up the process. Jim did hear one new piece of information that he tucked away.

"General Hood's big rebel army is on the loose and heading this way!" the post commander told Colonel Campbell. "We thought this was just a raid by Forrest, but he is just out scouting for General Hood. We don't know whether they are headed to Nashville or Memphis, but everyone down here has been ordered to retreat. After Ft. Pillow, all our colored troops are being replaced with white troops, and all the colored troops are being sent to Memphis to defend that city if he goes in that direction. You men should head north with us and then ride with our men to Memphis when we are relieved. The whole department is being reshuffled!"

Jim certainly did not follow all of this, but he knew the words, "big army" meant something. He also had heard of Memphis and knew it to be a large city on the Mississippi River. He couldn't imagine going there, but he knew that as long as he stayed close to Lieutenant Green, he would probably see it soon.

Within the hour, they were moving north again, leaving the bridge and blockhouse burning behind them. They could see Confederate riders on the other side of the river almost as soon as the flames took hold.

All along their retreat north toward Nashville, they sensed the Rebels hot on their trail. The force Jim had joined was small compared with his brother's surrendered men at Ft. Henderson, so he never felt very safe. As they moved north, more and more retreating men joined them. Cavalry, which Jim was learning meant men on horses; artillery, which meant men manning the rolling cannons; and infantry, the soldiers who seemed to do the marching, were all interspersed with wagons of all descriptions and sizes. There were officers and other soldiers on horseback and ox-pulled carts with bigger cannons and all manner of cooks and clerks and just about anyone that was part of the huge Union Army. All moving north, all getting out of the way of the big rebel army that was coming fast, with Forrest at its tip.

Jim always kept Lieutenant Green in his sight. He did not get too close, for that meant getting close to Colonel Campbell again, but he was able to keep up in the crush of men and animals easily. No one moved too fast. He marveled at the rich countryside and farms they passed. More than once, he saw young boys manning plows in the fields on either side of them, watching their progress down the dusty roads.

Finally, on the outskirts of a little town called Franklin, Lieutenant Green came to him. He brought another man with him, a sergeant named Nash, dark-skinned like his brother but with only three stripes to his brother's five.

"Jim, this is Sergeant Nash. He is with the 68th USCT detached from Memphis. He will be going back there once we get to Nashville. Stay with him now, and if you want to join the army, do so with him. I've explained your situation, given Sergeant Nash my information. When we reach Memphis, as I'm sure that is where I will eventually be, I will look you up. Your brother, Jesse, was one of our finest soldiers, and I owe it to him to look after you. Sergeant Nash comes highly recommended and will be a good guide for you."

Jim shook Sergeant Nash's hand, thanked Lieutenant Green and watched the kind man rejoin his party and ride away.

"Jim, welcome to the Fighting 68th," Sergeant Nash said. "A few of us are staying here in Franklin, preparing some earthworks. The lieutenant says you may want to join up. Says your brother was a sergeant major. All that correct?"

"Yes, sir," Jim said. Jim knew what "earthworks" meant now. He had seen the strength of the fort his brother had built, but he also knew they had weaknesses, the largest being who commanded them.

"Well, let's start there. I'm not a sir. That's for officers. I'm a sergeant, and that is just as important. Anyone you see that has stripes on their arms, you say, 'Yes, Sergeant' and 'No, Sergeant.' Understand?" Jim did, nodding with a "yes, Sergeant" thrown in.

"You'll do just fine. Now, you come tent with us tonight. I see you already have a uniform coat. We'll get you a cap soon and some new shoes and pants. There will be gear aplenty as all these soldiers come through here on the retreat to Nashville. In the morning, we will start digging earthworks for the soldiers that will have to defend this place. That will be your first job as a soldier."

Chapter 10

A Long Walk

By the third night, Jesse was miles south, deep in rebel-held Alabama.

Luckily, he had learned to read while in the Union Army. A group of missionaries from Boston had come down south to run a school for the black soldiers in Pulaski. They had moved back to Nashville as rumors of Forrest's raids had gotten steadily more credible. Their efforts were now paying dividends for Jesse as he read Lieutenant Green's note.

He had dared not pull out the slip of paper until he knew he would not be seen by the guards. Everyone around him was asleep, and the guards kept to themselves by their own fire many yards away. They didn't seem too worried about anyone escaping, as there was really nowhere to go. The danger of being caught as an escaped slave here was just as bad as the consequences of where they were going. Most had resigned themselves to their fate. It was a skill learned from a lifetime of servitude, and they slipped back into it easily. At least on the surface.

Jesse heard every rustle of the paper, magnified to his ears, as he unfolded it.

> "This man is Jesse Coffee, Sergeant Major of the 110th USCT. Trust him. He is an expert in fortification construction and a leader of men."
>
> Lieutenant Howard Green
> 110th USCT, Company B
> Commanding

Jesse folded the paper back carefully and slid it in a small oilskin pouch he carried in his pocket to keep it safe from the weather. As Lieutenant Green had anticipated, this letter, this note of confidence, could do wonders for Jesse at some point in his life. He had to trust that the time would come, that he would survive until then.

Over the last few days, the men began to settle more and more into looking to him and the other sergeants for guidance. Jesse had let them know to play along, to do the Rebels' bidding, and that at some point in the future, they would be able to strike back. But not now. They would lie low, biding their time.

Luckily, they had an Indian summer. They were moving south, so the shorter days of November were easier than they could have been. None of them had gotten to keep their blankets, and what footwear they had left fell apart as they walked the hard, red clay roads of Alabama. The flat terrain was turning mountainous now as they crossed the foothills of the Appalachian Mountains. Jesse had studied maps with his officers, and he knew they would soon pass these for the lowlands of the coast.

Jesse loved to look at terrain. He could read water flow in the valleys, see the contours of the hills and know whether it would be higher or lower just around the next bend. It was his gift, honed from a lifetime of work under Marse. But more than that, he could feel the earth and know if the ground was good for digging earthworks or for tunneling. As they had built Ft. Henderson, he knew he had done well. What he had not known was just how destructive and dangerous artillery shells exploding at their backs could be. No one in their fort had known that.

Most civil war battles were stand-up affairs; lines firing at each other on open ground. None of their officers had really been in a fight before, and no one had told Jesse how the attack would come. He would know better next time, and he knew that he could use this to his advantage.

Dawn brought more walking. They stopped in a little town

called Elyton that smelled of sulphur and smoke, then continued a long climb over a mountain that Jesse knew was red with iron. Up one hill and over the next, on and on. Days turned into a week, and still, they trudged south. They had seen Forrest's guards replaced with the Home Guard, old men and boys with fearful looks in their eyes at so many negroes in one place, their fingers always on their triggers. But none of the Union men walked out of the march. Once again, nowhere to go.

The earth turned color. Jesse noticed the soil turning black and the hills flattening. The weather was warmer as they moved into December. As they camped, the men slowly turned their blue coats to brown by boiling them at night with acorns and walnuts. They no longer looked like soldiers, and the meager rations they were given were slowly turning the men to skeletons before Jesse's eyes.

Many days, he walked with different groups of his former company sergeants, just to make sure they understood that even though they were prisoners, they still, at least to Jesse, were part of the Union Army. They knew it wasn't right they were being treated like slaves and not prisoners of war, but this was not a fight any of them had joined without that knowledge anyway.

Some days, he walked with Adler and Lucius, the two men that had been in the tower that last day with his brother. He asked them many questions about Jim, and it was reassuring to him they had taken to his brother and had seemed, through the accident of fate, to have gotten him out of this mess by sending him to see poor Tom.

"Jesse." They all spoke with first names now to keep from getting a rifle butt to the back by using rank. "The look on your face when you saw your brother walk out of that fort with the officers was priceless." Lucius said. "We wondered if you just had not had time to see the boy. But was it more than that?"

"Brothers, I'll confess, I was shocked." Jesse hesitated to tell the story as he still blamed himself for the loss of Ft. Henderson. "But I had another reason. Jim told me about the Yankees' ruse when he got back from walking the colonel around the Reb lines. And I hesitated. I didn't fully believe him. If I had listened to my own brother, which a big brother ought to have done, we might be free men even now."

Those words came hard to Jesse, who was not a man to show weakness. But it was important to come clean to these two men, the only two who had gotten to know his brother, even a bit.

"I thought I knew everything, and here was this wisp of a knucklehead brother telling me something not even our Colonel had recognized," Jesse said. "I still can't believe it, but I saw it with my own eyes."

"Don't worry, Jesse," said Adler, who was actually the oldest of all three of the men, even though he was just a private. "God didn't make us to believe our younger brothers. It takes years before they grow up to be us. Oh, we love 'em, but it's hard to see them as full-grown men even when they are."

"One thing's for sure, though," Jesse said, "He's in a lot better spot than we are. At least, I hope we meet again someday. I know I will never go back to that forsaken place we called home, so besides that, I don't know how I will ever find him again. Maybe he will head to Louisiana after this war to try to find our Momma, like I aim to do. I can't imagine the south will win this war if the best they have to guard us are these old men." He jerked his hand at an old rebel, huffing and wheezing and using his rifle as a crutch as they walked. Some of the guards were in much worse shape by now than the prisoners.

Finally, one day, they reached a riverbank, mosquitos everywhere, and were herded into a small stockade area that housed other black men. Like them, these men had been soldiers for the North at some point. If you looked closely, you could discern the remnants of their uniforms.

As the two groups mingled, they began to talk. Pretty quickly, Jesse was introduced to a big man with a long hardwood staff. The man had also been surrendered and was on the long march to Mobile.

"Name's Judas," the big man said to Jesse. "I was a sergeant in the garrison at Ft. Pillow. We lived what ya'll been hearin' about."

Judas had hooded eyes, and a scar ran down his cheek from eye to chin. It had not healed well. "Judas Pettigrew. I've seen it all, and I'm done with it all, and I don't mind telling you that you don't be trying to pull any rank on me or mine. You toy soldiers ain't been through what we have, and you and me might both be black, but I'm not your subordinate nor your equal."

Jesse was taken aback by the bluntness of Judas. His outstretched hand was ignored, and he let it drop. Judas was clearly older than him and clearly bigger and stronger – and clearly of his own mind. He was making sure right off the bat that even though Jesse outranked him in the old Union Army, he did not outrank him here.

Judas continued, "I'm the big boss man of this camp." He said it flatly, almost with no emotion, but Jesse could sense his power and might in those few words. "You do what I tell you, and you will do fine. You try to get in my way, or in my way regarding one of the men here, and I will crush you. You will spend your last days in the rottenest hellhole on God's earth. You understand, Sergeant Major?" He spat the last word and Jesse noticed that as they spoke, they had been surrounded by a dozen huge, muscled men.

Jesse opened his mouth to speak, but before any words came out, Judas swept a full blow with his powerful hand right across Jesse's face, crushing him to the ground. He saw Lucius and Adler run to his aid and watched them be felled as well. They all lay in the mud, and to add ignominy to insult, Judas stepped on Jesse's back and pushed him deeper into the stinking mud and bellowed, "All you new men. I'm Judas Pettigrew. I am the boss of this camp. I will eat any man who crosses me for breakfast and have his best friend for dessert. You listen from now on to me and to my chiefs. You do like we say, and you'll have no trouble. But you cross me, and I will break you into tiny pieces."

All the new men had crowded around now, but no one stepped forward to defend Jesse. They all registered shock, and soon resignation, as Judas continued to grind Jesse into the mud. "Now, if you believe what I say, go over there and get you some soup. And with that first bite, know you're mine, and that I am the big boss, and your life is in my hands now."

The big staff cracked down on Jesse's head. The lights went out.

Chapter 11

Spies

Jim's hands hurt. He had been shoveling for four straight days, digging trenches on the outskirts of this beautiful Tennessee town, while a flood of refugees streamed past on the road from the south.

Today, however, was his day of rest. He asked permission of Sergeant Nash and took off to town to borrow a fishhook from someone, and maybe a piece of line, and he was going to go back to that little stream he saw north of Franklin and catch something fresh. He had fished all his life on the banks of the Tennessee, and he was longing for some catfish. Or crappie. Whatever he could get his hook set in would do.

He wandered up the main street, passed the little town circle and all its Sunday commotion, and took a turn down a side street. He saw two white ladies struggling with their gate, and even though he knew he smelled worse than death just now, he offered to help them with it. The older woman accepted his offer, as they were hurrying to church.

Jim tipped his new Union Soldier's cap and pulled at the gate. He could immediately see that it had shifted and just needed a little tightening to be set right.

"Ma'am, I'm trying to go fishing down at the creek over there, but I have no hooks. If I might be so bold, I would be happy to fix your gate while you're at church for the use of a hook and some line, beggin' your pardon, Ma'am." Jim stepped back into the street. He had never spoken so boldly to a white lady before.

The women looked at one another. It was different times. But with the captain off at war, no one was around to do these small chores anymore.

"My name is Mrs. Richardson, young man. You may do the work, and as your reward, my daughter, Mattie, will go inside and fetch you a fishhook and some line from the captain's stores. I believe he even has a serviceable pole that you can use." She did not say this haughtily, as he assumed she would. But as a person to another person. He remembered that Sergeant Nash had told him Franklin had been behind Union lines for most of the war, and these people were used to Yankees, although not necessarily colored soldiers.

Mattie Richardson appeared to be his age, and she whirled and dashed inside and was back in a few minutes with a good pole, line and several hooks. She even brought a small keeper basket in case he had some luck.

"And I will have you know, young man, that is not a creek, as you call it, but our river. The Harpeth River. You will be glad to respect it as such, and please be so kind as to bring us back a small portion of your catch. The captain was such a fine fisherman before the war…" Her voice trailed off, and she looked past him.

He doffed his hat once again, assured her that he would, and watched as they turned the corner to walk the two blocks to the square.

Jim settled in to work on the gate. Using the back of one hook as a screwdriver, adjusted the mechanism so that it was good as new. He took the gear and headed to the river, his spirits the highest they had been in a year. The Indian Summer helped; the weather was fine. He was in the Union Army now – a free man who had a day off to go fishing.

He reached a spot that looked promising: a large mansion behind him on a hill with a beautiful gate out front; a nice path down to the fairly small "river," which was nothing like his mighty Tennessee; and plenty of soft earth for worms. He dug in and before long had a handful of bait. He tied a little strip of cloth to the line as a float, squeezed a sinker he had sliced off a lead Minnie ball and bit it on the line with his teeth at what he estimated was just the right depth and commenced fishing.

Jim could hear the rumble of wagons on the bridge downstream. He was just in sight of the big fort and its menacing cannon on the north shore, but he seemed far away from war. The first bite pulled in a nice, white-bellied cat, and several more followed. His basket filled over the hours as he lay by himself on the gentle bank. All the troubles of the world slipped away, as they are wont to do when fishing. He began to feel himself doze.

He awoke to a rustle. Not a loud noise, but he had heard the sound before, and the hair on the back of his neck stood up. He knew he was down in the grass, and fairly hidden by the bank, so he stayed very still, just opening his eyes and raising his head just a fraction.

There they were again. Confederate scouts, this time on horseback, just on the other side of the small river, watching the fort and the bridge. Two of them, one with some kind of spyglass. They spoke quietly to themselves and just stood there, horses' feet in the water, in the shade of the bank from the afternoon sun, almost invisible. And twenty feet from Jim. Again.

He lay still, pole in the water, a basket of catfish that he very seriously wanted, and two enemy soldiers close by. He had been through this before, and he began to think about what to do. His best course, he decided, was to lie low and then report this to the next Union sergeant or officer he ran into in town. He would speak forcefully this time, however.

He never got the chance. A rifle cracked the air, and he felt the rush of the wind as a ball passed over his head. It struck one of the horsemen in the shoulder, knocking him off his horse and into the water. He floated like a dead man. His partner, clearly spooked, grabbed the reins of the dead man's horse and took off galloping through the river and disappeared in seconds.

Jim looked up and saw the puff of smoke from the fort. What a shot that was! That must have been five hundred yards away. Jim had seen Marse hunt … but never a shot like that!

So, the fort knew the two men had been there. That relieved Jim of that responsibility. But Jim could see no movement from the fort in this direction. That meant they probably thought they just scared the men away and had not actually hit anyone. But that was not true. Blood started to float past Jim from the dead man.

Jim waded out toward him. He was not big and certainly no bigger than Jim, but when Jim reached for him, he was also not dead. He rolled, water spewing from his mouth, and his eyes opened wide. He saw Jim, the color of his skin, the blue of his cap, and feebly tried to push away. Jim pulled him to the shallow bank, both still in the water. He felt his waist for a pistol and finding one, pulled it from the holster and set it behind him on the bank, taking time to hide it so the young man, if he recovered quickly, would not find it easily. His blood-soaked tunic continued to ooze blood from his wound, and Jim felt him go limp again in his arms.

With the soldier now safe from drowning, Jim pondered his next move. The soldier lay on top of Jim on the bank, pulled there by his efforts to save him. But this presented Jim a challenge. What did you do in a situation like this? Should he let him die? Was he supposed to save an enemy soldier? Jim didn't know. But he did know he had to do something, and he decided to get him to town and a doctor's care. It seemed the right thing to do.

He clambered out from under him and searching around for some fallen limbs in the tangled undergrowth on the bank he found two fairly long, straight branches. He quickly stripped off his new blue jacket and slipped the sleeves through the sticks and rolled the unconscious Confederate onto his coat. He buttoned the buttons around the wet soldier and used the boy's own belt to secure him even tighter to the sled. Then he grasped the branches with his sore but strong hands and pulled him up the shallow bank and onto the path leading to town.

As luck would have it, Jim saw the Richardson ladies as he

entered Franklin. They were some of the first from church that day and were walking toward him as he pulled the soldier down the street. He was bursting with sweat and exertion and practically collapsed at their feet as they realized what he was doing. Mrs. Richardson sprang into action. From the blood, it was impossible to tell if the soldier was North or South, but as Jim watched her dress the wound, he knew she did not care. He was just a boy, dying from a gunshot wound, and she was going to help.

"Mattie," she spoke firmly, "run to town and get the doctor. We will be right here. This boy should not be moved anymore."

She saw the look on Jim's face. "No, Jim, you did the right thing, getting him to town. I don't know how you came across this poor unfortunate soul but thank heavens you did. You might have saved his life." Jim relaxed, and as he caught his breath, he began to help her. She placed a thick strip of cloth torn from the hem of her dress over the wound and had Jim hold it, pushing hard. He saw the color was starting to come back in the boy's face as Mrs. Richardson staunched the flow of blood.

"He's a rebel, Ma'am." Jim said.

"Well, so, he is. Did you shoot him?" Mrs. Richardson asked.

"No, ma'am, shot from the fort. He was out scouting, I think they call it. And he came up on me while I was dozing. Him and another fellow that got away."

"Did the soldiers from the fort see him?" she asked, a sideways look at Jim.

"No, ma'am, not that I know. I think they just shot to scare them away, and then, the horses were gone in a flash, and I'm not sure they saw him fall."

"You know my son is a Confederate officer, don't you, Jim?" she asked him again, a little bolder while still tending the wounded boy.

"Yes, ma'am," Jim said.

"And if this boy were my son, another mother would be tending these wounds. What do you think about this boy surviving, just to go into a northern prison camp to die?"

Jim hadn't considered that. He really hadn't considered much, just thought to save another person. It began to dawn on him what Mrs. Richardson was asking him to do.

"Ma'am, do you want me to not tell?" Jim asked. He had always done what white people said, unquestionably, but now, he was a free man, and he was being asked what he wanted to do, not told what to do. He was unsure of himself.

"Let us see how events unfold, Jim, before you have to make any hard decisions. The Lord puts questions before us and, sometimes, He gives us the answers, and sometimes, He does not. We must make the right choice. But sometimes, he solves the dilemmas for us."

"Yes, ma'am," Jim said, somewhat relieved to momentarily be off the hook. He concentrated on helping her save the boy, who still lay unconscious on his traverse.

Mattie came running with the doctor and a group of people from the town. Jim slowly faded into the background, not needed like before. He hoped the boy would live. He truly did. But it was out of his hands now. He was comfortable in his decision, but still shaken from the experience. He decided to walk back and get his fish. As he backed away, Mrs. Richardson whispered something to Mattie, and she came to his side.

"Mama says you did a brave thing today, Jim. Come by tomorrow, and we will have your nice coat ready for you, clean as can be. And be sure and drop us off a fish on your way back, and we will give you some nice warm bread. Thank you, Jim. That could have been my brother." With that, she touched his arm lightly and was gone, back in the crowd.

Jim walked back to the bank, retrieved his fish and gear, and pulled the pistol from its hiding place. He had seen Marse's pistol before, and this looked a lot like that one. He put it in the basket under the fish and headed back to Sergeant Nash, wondering what he would say. But one thing was certain … he always seemed to run into Rebels, and he was keeping that pistol.

Chapter 12

The Pact

Jesse awoke in a shabby tent, tended by Lucian. His head pounded.

"Hold still, Sarge, I mean Jesse," Lucian said in a whisper. "You took a good one to the head, and we need to see how you are."

The memory of the last humiliation came flooding back to Jesse. He had not had a chance to process that there was a new situation for him to understand and that he was at the center of it.

"What was that all about, Lucian?" Jesse asked.

"Well, it appears that the Rebels here are pretty much on their last legs, but they mean to fight it out. So, they have us 'slaves' building their fortifications down here. We are in a little town called Blakeley, almost to Mobile. But the Rebs are short of manpower, and they have this 'big boss' running the show. They don't have enough men to guard us all, so they pay the Boss's gang with extra food and better shelter, and they are our overseers. They are working us pretty hard. But you can tell none of them knows much about fortifications. Or building anything, for that matter. That landing out there is as shoddily built as anything I've ever seen. You wouldn't have let us get away with that for a second!" Lucian said.

Lucian always was a talker, and at the moment, Jesse's head just hurt.

Jesse started work the next day. He and Lucian and Adler had the job of running a tired-looking set of mules to pull logs cut down by the other soldiers and slaves in the swamps around Blakeley. The cypress logs they cut were heavy and hard to handle, but Jesse had never seen such solid wood to build with. He was used to working with pine from the forests of north Alabama. It was soft and easy to work, but he had seen what shell fragments had done to it. It just could not stand up.

This gave him an opportunity to understand the ground they were fortifying, and to see what the Confederate engineers had laid out and what the boss was trying to build. It was a strong position. One side anchored on the top of a high bluff overlooking a swamp that led to the Blakeley River. Deep ravines cut the landscape and provided covered avenues for Union troops to get close, but all the trees in those ravines were being cut and pulled to the high places where the fortifications lay. When finished, there would be a lot of killing ground for Union troops.

An idea slowly formed in Jesse's mind. Just as he was an expert at building fortifications, he realized he was just as much an expert at finding their weak spots. He saw right away there was a gap between Redoubts Two and Three that was built all wrong and could be a way to storm the defenses should it ever come to that. He watched it every day as they pulled logs from the bottoms, fighting mosquitos by the cloud-full and snakes everywhere. The mud stank, and the gas from the disturbed mud smelled of sulfur and dung.

He did his work and thought about how to gain his revenge but mostly how to help a Union Army that, if all this activity was predicated on it, would arrive soon enough. A Union victory would be the best way to settle his score.

Jesse's work area mostly put him on the north side of the works, close to the bluffs. He realized his biggest challenge, should a Union Army appear, was how to get his knowledge out of the Confederate lines and into the Union lines. It would be impossible for a man to make it through the killing fields between the armies. He had to find another way. Or perhaps build it.

He spoke to Lucian and Adler that night about his plan.

"Boys, I have an idea. It is dangerous, maybe deadly, but we are still soldiers, and we must still fight for the Union even though we are in these straits. And we are going to need help, men we can trust, who will also risk all for the cause."

Lucian and Adler looked at him in disbelief.

"Jesse are you serious?" the older Adler said. "They almost killed you once. If you try anything like this, big boss will kill you, and if he doesn't, the Rebs will."

"We are soldiers. We are men. We are no longer slaves. But we must think like soldiers, think like men. We make our own choices. Sure, we have a tough lot we have been dealt, but we can make the best of it--not by having it easy on ourselves but by making the decision to be men. To be soldiers. Our time will come again, and I want to be ready." Jesse could feel his passion rise. He prayed his two closest companions in this nightmare would join him.

Lucian spoke first.

"Jesse, I will follow you. And I know men who will. But we need a good plan, and I believe you're just the man to come up with it. I've had a taste of freedom, and I'm not satisfied to give it up. Having a plan that will get me back there quicker, even with death as a free man as the result, is better than living like a beast of burden again any day. Lead, and I will follow, and I will find you others to help."

Adler looked at his mates with disbelief. What they were discussing was crazy, sure to get them killed. But anything was better than this. You couldn't taste freedom and then easily suffer bondage.

"I'm in," he said. "I need a dream, no matter how crazy. Count me in."

The three men shook hands, their agreement complete, soldiers again.

Chapter 13

Nashville

The feel of a freshly cleaned coat was one Jim was not sure he had known since his mother left. For a month, Jim dug and fished, fished and dug, and never in that time did he ever mention that wounded Confederate boy. Not to anyone.

It weighed heavy on him sometimes, not telling Sergeant Nash. But he had begun to like the Richardson ladies, and they kept him supplied with bread he took back to his messmates in the 68th, and he brought the Richardson's fresh catfish and bream. He knew his place with them and was always very respectful, but he always wondered if inside was a recuperating Rebel soldier.

In early November, word came that General Hood's Rebel army was on the move, and the target looked like Nashville. Sergeant Nash addressed the dozen men of the 68th on detail.

"Hood's on his way. Might come through here, might not. We have been ordered back to Nashville to begin digging the forts up there," he said with resignation. "Looks like we might never get to fight, just dig. But orders are orders, and we move in an hour. Get your stuff squared away."

He looked at Jim. "Any chance you can get one more loaf of that mysterious bread you always end up with?"

Jim smiled. He never told anyone where the meals came from.

"Sure, Sarge. Can I meet you at the Harpeth Bridge?" Jim said.

"We will wait for that, young Jim," Sergeant Nash smiled. "And I've requisitioned a rifle for you to carry, but before I do, I need to swear you in officially in the regiment. Will you raise your right hand? Gather 'round, men."

The other soldiers crowded around Jim, and he raised his right hand and swore allegiance to the United States of America and to its defense. He now could count himself a soldier of the Union Army, and he took pride in his steps as he headed one last time to the Richardson's. The rifle, heavy on his shoulder, and the Rebel pistol on a string around his neck and under his coat, made him feel like a warrior. But as he walked up to the Richardson's back door and knocked, he was instantly a young boy.

Mattie answered the door, a surprised look on her face. Jim never came down at this time of day and never with a rifle on his shoulder and bedroll around his back.

"Are you headed to the war, Jim?" she asked.

"Yes, Ma'am," Jim said. "The sergeant sent me down to see if we could get one more loaf of that bread before we head to Nashville."

"But of course, Jim." She closed the door behind her as she scurried back inside.

Her mother reappeared with her.

"We want to thank you, Jim," Mrs. Richardson said. "We never had any Yankee patrols come by and ask about that wounded boy. When this terrible war is over, you always are welcome here."

Jim felt the welcome. He had never felt that from a white person before. It was a good feeling, one that he would keep tucked away in his heart.

"Thank you, Ma'am," he doffed his cap. "I might see you again in better days."

Jim rejoined his comrades and began the short march to Nashville. The road was in good shape, the weather was fine, and they marched with many more soldiers heading north. They trudged up and down small hills and wound around others. As they topped one hill in particular, the site of Nashville amazed Jim.

A great white building with huge white columns all around sat on top of a hill in the middle of the great sprawling city. Smoke from the hearths of thousands of homes swirled all around it. Nashville dwarfed the small towns and villages Jim had seen. Ringing it were more fortifications, black embrasures with cannons sprouting from them at every possible interval. One fort, however, caught his attention, and Jim saw Sergeant Nash speaking with one of their officers, who pointed in the fort's direction.

"We're heading over to that fort on the hill, men," Sergeant Nash said when he returned. "That's Ft. Negley, the key to the whole city's defense. That will be our home for a while."

As they marched onto the grounds of the fort, they walked past hundreds, maybe thousands, of black folks like him, camped all around the outskirts of the fort on the hill. They lived in tents and shacks that looked like they had seen better days. The road was muddy, as were all the fields around the fort. Mud created by the great mass of people who lived around the fort.

"You ever wonder where all our people have gone as they have escaped bondage? You're looking at it," Sergeant Nash said to them as they walked through the sprawling camp and up the hill to the fort.

They passed hundreds of black men moving up and down the hill to Ft. Negley. Sergeant Nash stopped to talk to one group and get the lay of the place. The soldiers crowded around to hear.

"Welcome to our fort," the worker said. "We have been working up here for months, and Captain Morton says it's the biggest fort he has ever built. We work here every day, and we aim to make it the strongest place we can build for our new freedom."

"Do they pay you to work up here?" Sergeant Nash asked.

"Oh, some of us, they do," the worker responded. "But most of us come up here to work to show that we mean to help in any way we can. This is our war more than theirs, and just 'cause only a few of us, like you boys, get to carry a gun and wear the blue, it doesn't mean that the rest of us can't pitch in. Most of us have families out here in the camp, so we just can't up and leave them, but when we ain't workin' for what pay we can get around here, we all take some time to work on our fort. It's our fort, no matter what you might hear. We aim to make it so strong that the Rebels never get close to our families again."

He gestured to a graveyard built in a low area on the side of the fort, makeshift crosses planted in large numbers.

"Many of us have given our lives in this place to keep ourselves free. We've suffered almost six-hundred dead building this fort. But we have built a place of safety for ourselves and our families."

Jim looked up at the structure, crowning the largest hill in sight. Its stout walls spoke for the man. Compared to Ft. Henderson, this place looked like a castle, not just a small earthen dam. Enormous gates, blockhouses, huge cannons jutting from the sides. The stone walls showed the strength of the place. Jim had seen what the Rebel cannon could do at Ft. Henderson, but he knew those cannons could not make a dent in this awesome place.

He swelled with pride. His people had built this place. If they could do that, they could do anything. He wore the blue and carried a rifle over his shoulder, and it would be his job to defend this place and keep his people safe. If only Jesse could see Ft. Negley! How proud he would be.

The men trudged up the hill, and Sergeant Nash saluted the smartly turned-out guard at the huge gate. As Jim entered, he could see how solid it was inside, too. No mere head logs here; this had places for the soldiers to stand and fire at attackers in almost complete safety. And the cannon inside were bigger than any he had ever seen. He understood why so many of the ex-slaves were camped outside. Ft. Negley bespoke safety and security for them.

Sergeant Nash gave the few men in his detail the night off after they reported to the fort commander and found out where they would bivouac.

"You boys stay up here on the hill," Sergeant Nash said, his voice changing to a more fatherly tone. "Down that hill toward town is a place called Smokey Row, loaded with all the devil's handiwork and not a place for you to be." Jim took notice and determined to stay away from a place filled with the Devil.

The Richardson's had supplied Jim several loaves of fresh bread, and Jim took one of the loaves and decided to walk through the small city set up outside the fort gates. It would be nice to walk through a town of people like him.

As it was evening, he strolled through the makeshift streets just as the workmen were coming home to their families. Wives were cooking over communal fires, children were playing and greeting their fathers as they returned from the day's toils, and the teenagers of Jim's age were strolling around talking and laughing. Jim had never seen such joy. No masters here. No threat. This was life as Jim had never dreamt.

At one such vignette, Jim stopped, just outside the firelight. A weary father returning home, a loving mother and small son smoothing a spot on a blanket for him to sit by the fire, a steaming plate of food scooped from the kettle onto a plate and placed before him. Smiles. Touch of human hands, hands weary yet loving, touching. Husband to wife. Father to son. Jim watched the father stretch out his legs as he enjoyed the food and relaxed in the love of his family.

The mother caught Jim watching them.

"Good evening, young soldier," she said. Jim was taken aback, glancing behind him before he realized she was addressing him.

"Good evening, Ma'am," he said shyly.

"Are you new here?" she asked. "I don't remember ever seeing you before. And a soldier in blue, too. I would have noticed you, I think." Jim saw the father smiling at his discomfort.

"I'm new, Ma'am. We just arrived today. I guess we are going to be part of the garrison at the fort for a while."

"Well, you might as well sit down and join us tonight. Lucy and I have been cooking on this stew all day, and we have just enough for you. I'm Mrs. Workman, and this here is my husband, Mr.

Workman. This is our son, TJ.

Jim opened his haversack and pulled the loaf of bread out. Mrs. Workman's smile widened. "That's just fine if you want to share that nice bread…"

Jim shyly looked at his feet, embarrassed to be talking to a woman, which he had rarely done since his Momma was taken. "My name is Jim," he finally said as he handed the loaf to her. He felt the sting of tears welling in his eyes as he looked on this family, the absence of which stung him deep down in his soul.

Mrs. Workman placed a gentle hand on his arm. He could feel the kindness in that touch. "Don't you mind, young Jim. We all have our stories. Not many of them are good. You just sit down here by the fire and rest yourself. Speak as you feel called, and don't let little TJ run you over too much."

TJ, who was small, active, had laughing eyes and the energy of a four-year-old, bounded over to Jim as soon as he sat down by the fire. He reached for Jim's soldier cap and pulled it onto his own small head. Jim laughed. He couldn't ever remember being around small children, and the joy and abandon of this little one filled a hole in his heart he did not know he had. With each bounce of little TJ on his lap, each peal of laughter, each wide-eyed look at Jim, he felt a small door in his heart open.

Next to the fire sat the family's home: the roof of a tent draped over a small frame of wooden supports. The door, tall enough for a person to stand up in yet also made of canvas, pushed open, and out stepped a girl of Jim's age. Time stopped. Maybe it was because TJ had opened some air into Jim's heart, or maybe it was because Jim had never really been around any girls his own age, or maybe it was because the girl, Lucy, the daughter, he supposed, was so beautiful. Whatever the cause, Jim stopped playing with TJ, his mouth hung open, and he could not take his eyes off the girl.

She wore a flowered dress and had flashing eyes and delicate features. There was something about the way she moved as she carried something to her father and … Pow! Jim felt the hard punch of her father right in the shoulder. It broke the spell – but just for a moment.

“What are you lookin’ at, Boy?!” Lucy’s father said, though more playful than angry. He knew the effect of his daughter’s beauty.

Jim felt the heat rush to his face and dropped his gaze quickly back to TJ, scuffing the boys’ hair. But when he glanced back up to Lucy, he saw her eyes on him also. Lightning and electricity passed between them, and everyone, save maybe for little TJ, knew it.

Chapter 14

Fort Negley

November brought an Indian summer to Tennessee. Jim drilled with the garrison of Ft. Negley during the day and spent all the time he could with the Workman family in the evening. His friendship with the family grew, and he spent as much time as Mr. Workman would allow with Lucy, though never very far from her protective father's view.

Mr. Workman and hundreds of other freed black men worked on the fort. Rumors ran rampant that the Confederate Army was on the march to Nashville, and Jim watched the workers struggle to get the fort ready for the day it's mighty walls and cannon would have to defend the city and the camp of ex-slaves. Men literally worked themselves to death. Disease ran rampant, stones crushed arms and legs for which little medical care could be provided, yet still the men trudged up the hill to work on the fort.

Jim pulled guard duty with Sergeant Nash one warm evening at the end of the month. As the sun came up, they watched riders scurry over the roads leading into Nashville. Columns of Union soldiers continued to march into the city. From their vantage point, they could see miles of earthworks being constructed. Trees were cut, houses that might give the approaching enemy shelter outside the fortifications were pulled down. The entire tent city for the freedmen was relocated for security behind the fort.

When their relief arrived, Jim walked down to the Workman tent. Lucy and Mrs. Workman were each rolling bandages as he approached. As was his custom now, Jim sat with them for a few minutes before he crawled into their tent to catch a few hours of sleep after his all-night guard duty. But today seemed different.

You could not help but feel the buzz of anticipation throughout the camp.

"Jim, did you hear any news last night at the fort?" Mrs. Workman asked.

"I've never seen so much activity on the roads as I did this morning, Ma'am," Jim replied.

"What do you mean?" asked Lucy, glancing up from her work to look at Jim with her luminous eyes.

"It feels like it did when we came from Ft. Henderson after the capture," Jim said. "I can feel the shift, the panic in the air. I would guess that the Rebels are on the move."

"They came and got all the men very early today," Mrs. Workman said. "They are even pressing the black people in the city to come out and work on the forts."

Sergeant Nash had to give Jim a pass, a note in writing, that said he was allowed to be out of the fort and at the Workman's camp, for just such an event. Since Jim worked his guard shift all night, he slept during the day. If he was caught sleeping in their tent during the day by the press gangs without that note, he could be forced to go out and work on the fortifications for no pay.

Lucy put down her bandage roll, reached into the basket next to her and pulled out two biscuits for Jim.

"Your breakfast, Jim," she smiled. His hand brushed hers for just a second as he took them from her. He could still feel the energy pass between them.

"Thank you, Lucy," he said shyly. He spent a great deal of time with the Workmans, but he still could not bring himself to talk directly to Lucy other than in small phrases. Sometimes they stole glances at each other as he played with TJ or spoke with her parents. He could feel their love growing. Love. Jim didn't really understand that word, but he liked the feeling of it. He thought very little of anything but Lucy. It kept him awake on those long November nights of guard duty, walking the parapet of the fort or guarding the big gate. He imagined saying all kinds of things to her, but when he was with her, the words just would not come.

Jim ate, then excused himself and stretched out for a little sleep in their tent, lying down in the spot Mr. Workman slept in, now vacated while the man of the house was out building fortifications. He fell asleep almost instantly.

The sun was well past noon when he awoke to the sound of thunder. Must be a storm coming, he thought dreamily as he pulled himself from sleep. Lucy appeared at the tent opening.

"Cannon!" she said excitedly. "The Rebels are here, or at least close, and we can hear the cannon firing. All the folks say that it's coming from down around Franklin!"

Franklin. Jim suddenly thought of the Richardsons and their little house down in Franklin. He hoped they were safe.

They sat by the fire for a few minutes, listening to the big guns boom in the distance. Too far to see, but the noise rolled continually over the hills and did not stop. Jim had heard the cannon at Ft. Henderson, so he could gauge a bit how big this fight was, and he deemed it a big one.

"I need to get to Sergeant Nash," he said to the ladies. TJ had rushed to his lap as soon as he awoke, and he tousled the boy's hair. "TJ, you stick close to the tent today, you hear?" he said to the little boy. The excitement ran through him, and without thinking, he grasped Lucy's hand and held it.

"Please be careful, Jim," she said with tears in her eyes.

Jim sprinted to the fort and quickly found Sergeant Nash on the parapet. The smoke from the big battle at Franklin could now be seen rising in the air. Riders scurried everywhere in the city below, and many townspeople had made their way to the hill around Ft. Negley. They were listening intently to the sounds of the fight.

The sounds did not end until after nightfall. Jim and Sergeant Nash posted for duty at the big gate. By early morning, they could hear the sound of marching men coming up the road from the south. The Union Army was marching into the city! The Rebels must have won because the whole Union Army filled the road.

Chapter 15

Trust

For Jesse's plan to work, he had to earn the trust of the big boss and the Confederate engineers who oversaw the construction of the fort. Jesse learned they were working on the defense of the little town of Blakeley, Alabama, just north of the big port city of Mobile. This fort would defend the city from attack from the land, not the sea. It was to be a hundred times bigger than Ft. Henderson.

Luckily for Jesse, this was work he knew and knew well. He started with just a crew of his own former soldiers clearing timber from in front of the trenches, cutting the big logs for use in the forts and adding the tops of the trees to interlace into impenetrable abatis in front of the lines. The Rebel engineers walked the line and studied the terrain as the fields were cleared.

Jesse had to find a way to get noticed. The men chopped trees down with axes all day, then another gang hooked chains on the logs and dragged them to one of the roads. Once the logs were stacked by the road, another group would use a pulley to hoist the logs onto a cart that would haul the wood to the staging areas behind the line of redoubts being built across the hills.

The hard part was getting the logs positioned beside the carts. It took a lot of brute strength to get the logs stacked and lifted so the chains could be wrapped around them for the lift into the cart. Many men had crushed their hands trying to maneuver the logs onto the carts. Once a man's hand was crushed, he became almost useless.

An idea popped into Jesse's head. If he could fasten a metal joint to a pole, then attach a large arm or hook to it, then he could manhandle the logs without having to slip hands under it. This simple invention could save a great deal of time and effort and make the work go smoother and safer. As Jesse swung his axe all day, he puzzled out the design in his head.

Finally, he thought he had it figured out. But he could not just go to one of the white Rebel engineers with his idea. No, he had to give the idea to the big boss and let him take credit for it. This had to be his first step.

That evening, he approached the fire the big boss and his men claimed as their own. It was the largest fire and the best equipped, with an iron grate and cantilever for cooking over. Jesse and his men were still using forked branches cut and staked on either side of their small fires.

Jesse was immediately recognized, and one of the bosses' men cracked him on the side of the head with a stave for daring to approach their fire. It knocked Jesse to the ground. The big boss sauntered over and stood looking down at Jesse.

"What do you want, Boy?" the big boss asked.

"I know a way to get the logs on the cart without anyone getting hurt," he said.

The Boss roared, "What do I care if anyone gets hurt?!" he scoffed. "That's what you men are here for, to work and to die!"

"But every time someone gets hurt, they miss work. I can help you keep more men working, and that means more labor for you." Jesse said.

The big boss thought a second, then relented. "Ok, show me."

Jesse stood, brushed himself off and walked over to the big fire. "I need to borrow this spit for just a second," he said. He looked down at the iron cantilever sitting over the fire. The metal was very hot. "Can I pull it away from the fire and let it cool down?"

The big boss looked around at his henchmen and laughed. "No, Boy, if you want to show me, you work with it while it's hot. I know you think you're better than me, so let's see if you have the guts to do that."

Jesse stared into the big boss's coal-black eyes and saw he meant it. Jesse knew this man was beyond cruel. Years of doing the white man's bidding had made him view treating black men as anything more than mules a foreign concept.

Jesse pulled off his shirt and ripped it in two. He used the cloth to protect his hands from the heat of the iron as much as possible.

He reached for the stave that the man had used to knock him to the ground. When the man hesitated to give it up, the big boss said, "Go ahead, give it to him."

Jesse took one arm off the hinge of the cantilever and placed it against the long stave.

"If I attach a hook here and sharpen the other end here, a man can stick the point in a log. Then the arm here," he pointed to the smaller end of the hinge, "will force that hook into the log like so. Now, you have leverage on the log, and I can move it anywhere I want, from the safety of the long pole. Now, my hands are safe, and I can move the log by myself." Jesse's hands began to blister as he held the hot metal hinge just so against the stave. He would not take his eyes off the big boss. He smelled his own flesh as it sizzled.

The big boss just stared at what Jesse was describing. He was not a dimwitted man. Though cruel, his brain was sharp, and he had the sense to know that he was looking at a good idea.

"Tomorrow, you come with me to the blacksmith, and let's try this out. If it works, it will be my idea to show the white folks, but it will get you off log duty and to something a little better. Deal?" the big boss held out his hand to Jesse's blistered fingers.

"Deal," said Jesse.

Chapter 16
Assault!

The Indian summer had ended, and the cold north wind blew at Jim's back.

Jim sat atop the parapet of Ft. Negley, looking out at the Rebel lines. As far as he could see on this bitterly cold December day, the two lines, Union toward the city and Confederate ringing the city, sat staring at each other. Jim knew today was the attack. The Union Army was coming out of the trenches to drive the Rebels away.

Sergeant Nash had informed his small group of men they would be detailed as stretcher bearers to a Union Colored infantry regiment today in their advance to the Rebel works. Jim looked over his shoulder and saw Sergeant Nash gesture for him to join them, and together, their little group walked out of the gate toward the lines. Jim looked back toward the strong walls of the fort and felt sorry for leaving. But it felt good to be going on the attack against the Rebels.

At the base of the hill, they joined General Morgan's 1st Brigade of United States Colored Troops, as fine a body of Union soldiers that Jim had ever seen. They formed into line of battle. Jim and Sergeant Nash's detail took their places behind the men with the stretchers.

"Our job is to tend the wounded and get them back to our lines if they should fall." Sergeant Nash explained. "We will stack our rifles here by the hospital tent. You won't need them today. These fine men will break the Rebel line, and our job is to support them." Sergeant Nash was beaming. Never before had any of them, ex-slaves all, seen such a powerful group of black men. Colors flying, blue uniforms looking sharp and arrayed in order of battle, they looked invincible.

The bugles sounded all along the lines, and the cannon from Ft. Negley began the deadly work covering the advance of the Union troops. Shells from the fort roared overhead as they pounded the Rebel fortifications. Jim followed the men of his regiment to the front as they surged forward.

The regiments deployed to their right, wheeled in perfect order, and Jim could feel that they were past the outer line of Union works. They saw a small Rebel redoubt ahead. It began to fire on the front ranks, and Jim saw gaping holes splayed into the Union line. Despite the destruction, the Union men moved forward.

Faster now, Jim began to run. He saw some of the stretcher bearers begin to drop off to tend wounded comrades, but the troops moved forward in a blue wave. Jim focused on the cross belts lining the backs of the men ahead.

Jim watched many men fall to his right as the men directly facing the Confederate fort were pummeled again and again with shots and shells from the Rebel batteries. But the men Jim followed lapped around the fort; then, they were past it and into the Confederate line! They clamored down into the deep ravine of a railroad line, then up and out and formed up on the other side, ready to make the final charge. They were close to winning!

The bugle sounded, and off they ran, running as hard as they could, one unstoppable wave of proud Union men, colors flying overhead, bayonets gleaming on the rifles. They could see a gash in the earth in front of them, a few Rebel banners above it. As they came closer and closer, they knew they would overwhelm the defenders in this gallant charge of free black men.

Then, all hell broke loose. As one, the gash of earth to their front was filled with shooting, shouting men who rose from the earth and unleashed a storm of shot on the Union regiment. Jim noticed the shooting was also coming from behind them, from the redoubt they had bypassed. Those Rebel gunners had turned their cannons to the rear and were firing into their backs.

On the right, more Confederate troops fired into their unprotected flank. The Union forces were caught in a deadly crossfire. Blue figures crumpled onto the cold ground all around Jim. He saw Sergeant Nash direct them to start carrying the wounded back from the killing field.

Jim's eyes stung from the smoke. He heard the whistle of bullets flying by his head, sounding like swarms of angry hornets. Suddenly at his feet was a wounded man, blood pouring from his cheek where a bullet had ripped through flesh, exposing the teeth and bone beneath. Jim crouched beside him, wrapped one of Lucy's bandages around his bloody face, and began to lead him to safety.

When the line ahead broke, it was the Union soldiers who did the breaking, first in small groups, and then the whole regiment began to turn and run back toward the railroad cut. Their momentum carried Jim and his wounded soldier with them. The once-magnificent ranks of soldiers were shattered now. They were soon a mob hiding in the ravine trying to evade the deadly three-sided crossfire.

But it was not to be. The Rebel's line extended into the railroad cut, and they turned several artillery pieces onto the Union troops, firing directly down the ravine into the packed troops. The carnage was horrible. Men hugged the ground while officers and sergeants tried to bring order back to the chaos.

Small knots of men began firing back. Others scrambled over the dead and dying to pull themselves out of the deep ravine. Men hid under the dead, listening to the bullets rip into their stilled comrades. The dead piled so high, so fast, that they created a barrier to the incoming fire. After what seemed an eternity, the living were able to retreat out of the railroad cut and escape to the rear. Jim, though small, continued helping his wounded soldier. At last, they gained their own lines, back where they had started, but there were so few of them. They had failed.

That evening, the dejected soldiers sat around their fires.

"We weren't even supposed to come as close as we did to the Rebel lines today," Sergeant Nash said to Jim and the other men of the stretcher detail. "I heard this evening that we were just a feint attack, meant to trick the Rebs into staying put. The generals never thought we could get so far. They thought we would run at the first shots. We were a diversion, doomed to fail."

Knowing they had been sacrificed was hard to accept. The main attack took place on the other side of the Union line, and it had caused the Rebels to retreat. It did not help the morale of the black troops to know their attack was never meant to succeed. Of course, they knew they played an integral part in the overall plan, but they had suffered a terrible loss of brave men. They determined to make it up the next day.

They sat underneath the booming cannon of Ft. Negley throughout the night as the big guns threw shot and shell at the retreating Confederates. A fresh brigade of USCT, the 2nd now, passed through the lines, and the battered 1st Brigade watched sullenly as this new group of black soldiers took its place for the assault tomorrow.

Jim laid his head on his knapsack and waited for the sunrise.

Chapter 17

A Good Plan

Jesse sighted down the transom over the top of the hill that would someday be crowned by Redoubt No. 3. He had worked his way into the good favor of big boss and had ensured his two comrades, Lucian and Adler, had joined him. They made a good team.

As yet, the fortifications were manned only by a handful of Confederate military engineers and big boss and his work crews. Jesse and his men no longer looked like Union soldiers. Their uniforms had worn out in the hard climate of south Alabama, and they had been issued rough work clothes. Since they had at one time all been slaves, many of the men reverted back to their pre-war condition and accepted their fate.

But not Jesse.

He was still a soldier, and he made it known to Lucian and Adler and a small cadre that they would, in time, regain their former stature, and they would continue the fight. They would just do it in an unconventional way.

Ft. Blakely was more than ten times the size of Ft. Henderson back in northern Alabama. Nine hills surrounded the small landing on the side of the Blakeley River that led downstream to Mobile. Each hill would be crowned by a strong redoubt or fort. The difference between Ft. Henderson and these redoubts was that they faced only one direction, the direction from which the Union Army must advance. When the line was manned by Confederate troops, their backs would be to the river. That meant almost no chance of retreat.

Jesse knew that when the time came for the Union Army to attack these lines, the Confederates would defend this ground to the last breath. They would make the Union men pay with their lives. Jesse knew exactly how to even the odds, and he set about making sure his plan worked. It was slow and tedious and must never be compromised or he and his men would be hanged.

At the northern end of the fortifications, the last fort, Redoubt No. 1, pushed right up against a tall bluff overlooking a deep swamp filled with snakes and alligators and other things vile and deadly. The cliff and the swamp were naturally impenetrable, and the fort sited along the top of the ridge added the man-made horrors of overlooking cannon and rifle pits.

A shallow ravine passed between Redoubt 1 and 2, also situated on a small hill with steep sides and soon to be crowned and bristling with cannon and rifles. Jesse saw no way any man could get close to either of these formidable earthworks. The swampy ravine in front and between them was being cleared of cypress trees, and the long slow slope from the hill on the far side left no cover for the Union Army to advance.

Redoubt 3, the next in line, was a different story. Three ravines converged at the base of the fort. From the fort, you could see down the length of the left and right ravines. The center ravine, however, was hidden almost to the base of the hill by the side of the first ravine. Visually imperceptible, that small fold became the centerpiece of Jesse's plan.

Jesse heard the approach of the Confederate engineer officer and the big boss, and he backed away from the transom.

"This here is the crowning fort of this side of the line, Suh," Jesse heard the big boss say to the Confederate officer. That man looked tired and quite sickly. Jesse knew most of the really competent Rebel officers had long since been sent to other lines more threatened by the Union than here at Blakeley. No Union troops might ever even make it to this position. As a matter of fact, it was hard to believe that the war would ever reach this backwater. Blakeley was not a big town, actually just a small landing with a few warehouses and a mill.

"I'm sure it is fine," the Confederate officer said, looking around at the great scars of earth being thrown up on all sides by the black men. He saw only slaves, Jesse knew. The officer did not know he was looking at former Union soldiers, so he let his guard down. He barely looked through the transom at the developing fortifications.

"Perfect," Jesse said quietly under his breath, just out of earshot of the two men.

He watched the big boss make sweeping gestures, showing the cleared trees, the earth being piled, and the log structures being built behind the mounds of earth, the slowly forming embrasures. But Jesse knew the big boss was all talk. Sure, he was a bully and had the ear of the Rebel officers, but he did not know ground like Jesse did. Jesse knew that his secret was safe, for the time being.

Mosquitos swarmed around everyone as the day ended. The Rebel officer motioned for his horse and with a nod to the big boss, rode back toward the camp.

That left Jesse alone on the hill with the big man, and it was very tempting to take a swing at him, as Jesse felt that in a one-on-one fight, he could take him, but now was not the time. He had to think of the future.

He removed his battered hat and walked, head down, the perfect picture of a cowed subordinate with nothing but ingratiating intentions, toward the big boss.

"What do you think, Suh?" Jesse said in his perfectly innocent voice, honed sharply from years of having to report to white masters and foremen who always thought they knew more than him.

But the big boss did not get to where he was by being easily fooled. He looked searchingly at Jesse.

"You is up to something, ain't you, boy?" the big boss said. With the Rebel officer long gone now, Boss whistled loudly, and from behind the forming earthworks, two of his henchmen dragged a badly beaten Lucian toward Jesse. Blood trickled from his unconscious lips.

Jesse' eyes widened. Fear gripped him, and he could also feel his anger rise.

The men dropped Lucian on the ground at Jesse's feet.

"We didn't ask him nuthin', and he didn't offer nuthin.' I'm just telling you in the best way I know how to do what I say because I say it. I know you still think you're high and mighty, Mister Sergeant Major," the big boss spat those words at Jesse.

"But I will kill you and your friends and anyone else who I think is double-crossin' me. You do this job right, you might live. But make no mistake, I own you boy. I own you."

Chapter 18

New Friend

The second day of the Battle of Nashville saw the Rebels routed. The 2nd Brigade of the USCT lost more than two-hundred men in the assault, but in the end, Nashville was safe. The Confederate Army, or what was left of it, staggered back to Alabama. Jim took no part in the battle of the second day, though he, like many of the civilians and soldiers from the city, watched the whole thing.

Before Jim could get back to let Lucy and the Workmans know he was not hurt, Sergeant Nash and his detail were called out of the ranks for an additional duty. They formed up with several other men, almost a hundred laborers armed with picks and shovels, and set off following the advancing Union forces back down the Franklin Road.

They passed the carnage of battle, dead men and horses lying everywhere. The smell was overpowering, and carrion birds circled overhead.

But their duty was not to tend to them.

"Our job is to get to Franklin as fast as we can and help bury the dead down there from the battle two weeks ago," Sergeant Nash told the men. "The rumors are that the Rebs have left many of our boys unburied, and it's our job to get them in the ground before the hard frost."

More shovel and spade work for Jim. But he was looking forward to seeing the Richardsons again and seeing how they fared during the battle. He often thought of them and hoped they were spared.

The detail crossed the Harpeth River on the remains of the beautiful bridge, now almost completely burned by the retreating Rebels. The smell of death and decay hung over everything as they crossed into the town. As Jim came to the street where the Richardson's lived, he asked Sergeant Nash if he could go see them.

"Sure, Jim, just you be careful. This town is full of wounded Rebels, and they might not take kindly to seeing a lone black Union soldier so close on their heels. Meet us at the top of the hill; we won't be hard to find."

"And bring us some of that bread, Jim!" Sergeant Nash called. Clearly, he had not forgotten the delicious rolls the Richardsons had supplied them back in November.

Everything had changed since they were here last. All the fences were torn down for firewood. The streets were churned into masses of mud by the feet of two armies moving back and forth through Franklin in such a short time. First was the big battle at the end of November that they heard so clearly on Ft. Negley's high hill. Next, the Union retreated through the town, followed by the Confederates on their way north to Nashville. Two weeks later, the Confederates retreated through here, rapidly pursued by the Union Army. Now came the gravediggers, trying to clean up the human carnage before the ground froze for the winter.

The Richardson's house still stood, but it was in shambles. Jim walked up to the back door and saw buckets of blood-stained rags and the debris of wounded men everywhere. Blood darkened the back-door steps where he had asked for fishhooks just a few weeks prior.

"Mrs. Richardson," Jim called. He heard voices inside; then, Mrs. Richardson's face appeared at the door. She looked exhausted. Blood smeared her apron, but her kind face beamed when she saw Jim.

"Young Jim, you made it!" she exclaimed. She reached both her hands to his and shook them. "So many haven't made it, and I so hoped you would be spared. And now, perhaps you have come to repay our favors."

She pulled the door open, so Jim could see inside. The house was full of wounded men, Confederates mostly, being tended by Mattie and a young black boy about his own age.

Mattie glanced at Jim, smiled a weak smile, and went back to her duties, a bloodied rag in her hand that she used to mop the mouth of a freshly arrived soldier.

"Henry, come meet Jim," Mrs. Richardson went on. "He is a friend and a Union soldier. Perhaps Jim can help us get some food and some clean bandages for our wounded here. Jim, this is Henry. He came to us with my son's Confederate regiment, whose wounded now litter our floor once again."

Mrs. Richardson looked skyward. "Lord, please help us alleviate these poor boys' misery."

Henry stepped out on the back porch and shook Jim's hand. They were about the same age, same size, and they clasped hands easily. Henry guided Jim out back to a small shed, out of the bitter December wind.

"Jim, Mrs. Richardson and Mattie told me about you. I'm from Georgia, came over with two mules and a cart stolen from my master's property. Those mules and that cart and that master are long gone now. I've been here helping the Richardsons care for all these wounded men. I sure hope you have some connections to get us some supplies. There is just about nothing left here," Henry said.

"I'll see what I can do, Henry, but I'm nothing important in the Union Army. I've just been a part of it for a few months, but I will bring my sergeant down as soon as I can and see if we can get some help," Jim said. "My home was in Alabama, and I have no one left there. Just a brother, and he was captured a few weeks back. I don't know if he is even alive."

"I have family back in Georgia," Henry said. "But I don't know how I will ever get back there. I aim to do like you, join the bluecoats and maybe earn some money that way."

"Well, they feed us, but I haven't seen any money yet," Jim said. "But I usually get a warm place to sleep and for the first time in my life, I feel like I belong somewhere."

"I know the feeling, Jim," Henry said. "The Richardson's are nice people. They don't treat me like a slave. They have needed me badly the last few weeks. But their son, the captain, is getting stronger, and soon, he can start to help out more. We just don't know what the Yankees," Henry stopped and grinned, "I mean you folks, will do with him. You know, Jim, I've never met a Yankee soldier before who wasn't a prisoner or wounded. I never expected my first one would be black like me and my age, too!"

Henry went with Jim to meet Sergeant Nash, and they brought him down to meet the Richardson's. Sergeant Nash brought one of the white officers with him, and he began arranging for supplies. They were all soldiers, and both sides regularly helped with each other's wounded.

"Thank you, Jim," Mrs. Richardson said to Jim finally. "You have always brought us good luck."

She turned to Henry.

"Henry, I can't thank you enough. You have been a godsend to Mattie and me. And you're welcome to stay. But I can see you're itching to go with young Jim and start your new life. I say go with our blessings and our thanks."

Henry looked at Sergeant Nash and at Jim.

"Well, come on, son," Sergeant Nash said. "Might as well have one more," and Henry joined Jim as they walked back to town.

Chapter 19

An Exciting Journey

Henry and Jim became fast friends over the next month as they finished their duties in Franklin. They accompanied Sergeant Nash as he returned to his regiment, the 68th USCT, forming up in Memphis. It was a big secret where they were going, but with the Rebels run completely out of Tennessee now, it was anyone's guess.

The two boys were officially sworn in as privates in Company A of the 68th USCT. To Jim's surprise, his company commander was Lieutenant Green, with whom he had escaped Ft. Henderson. They stayed with Sergeant Nash and joined the rest of his squad of ten men. Lieutenant Green drilled the men continually. Jim and Henry became proficient at marching in the battle line and with company drill. They each carried long Springfield rifles, and they were issued new blue uniforms and caps.

"I think you boys are growing," Sergeant Nash said one day. "This regular food and exercise is good for you."

Henry good-naturedly punched Jim in the arm. "I'm still bigger than him, Sarge," Henry said, laughing.

"You're crazy," Jim said, laughing, too. Sergeant Nash was enjoying watching Jim come out of his shell. He had heard the boy talk about Lucy and the Workman family. He also knew that Jim had become separated from his brother at Ft. Henderson. Henry had done wonders for him.

Henry was so much more playful than Jim. Henry had a family that loved him back in Georgia and had grown up with his mother and father close, so Jim asked him a lot about what it was like to have grown up with his parents around. Jim, on the other hand, had Lucy. He had not been able to see the Workman family before he left for Memphis, so he had not told her goodbye.

Since neither boy could read nor write, Jim asked Sergeant Nash to send a letter to Mr. Workman in Nashville.

"Sure, Jim, I'll try, but they have no address, and the best I can do is try to send it to someone I know at Ft. Negley and see if they can find them," Sergeant Nash said. Jim's heart broke that Lucy was going the way of his Mother, perhaps lost to time and distance and circumstance.

By February, rumors flew that the 68th Regiment would join all the other regiments in Memphis, black and white, and steam south toward the Gulf of Mexico. They were forming up into an army under General Steele. It was exciting for Jim and Henry to be part of an entire division of black soldiers like themselves. The week they were to depart, all the USCT regiments formed up on the big parade ground and met their division commander, General Hawkins. All the officers of the division were white, but the soldiers and their sergeants were black like Jim. All the men swelled with pride. Jim could not hear what the general had said to them that day, but a copy was circulated around the regiment, and eventually, Sergeant Nash read it to them. Jim heard one thing … they would be boarding the big steam ships soon.

Jim's whole life he had seen the big ships cruising by his home on the river. He knew his Mother had been taken down river on one. Yes, he thought, this big ship will take me away from Lucy, but it might be taking him closer to finding his mother!

The boys boarded a steamer with a huge paddlewheel on the back, the "stern," they learned to call it. It puffed and chugged its way down the Mississippi River, past the old fort at Vicksburg, in a long convoy of other ships. It was a massive flotilla, and Sergeant Nash and Lieutenant Green let the boys stay on deck and watch the sights go by. Henry noticed Jim watching intently every time they went by a plantation or field with black workers.

"One of these days, I just think I might spot my Momma," Jim said when asked by Henry what he was looking for.

"That is a needle in a haystack!" Henry said. But he softened and told Jim he would help. Of course, they both knew that it was impossible, but Jim liked that his new friend cared enough to make the offer.

One day, as they chugged along, Jim and Henry saw a great white house rise from the riverbank. The word spread that this plantation was called the White Castle. Many black laborers worked its banks, and many women stood along the bank of the river, watching with pride as the black Union troops sailed past. Cheers always arose when the black folks, most still slaves, saw their own kind sailing past to deal death and destruction to the Rebels. They were so proud of their men!

Jim had studied every woman's face intently as they had sailed down the river. He looked for her hair, her eyes, the shape of her face, the tilt of her head. Here at White Castle, there were so many women, standing along the riverbank, his eyes hurt from the strain of concentration.

One woman caught his attention. Something about her dress, or the dignity with which she carried herself, or perhaps just a son's natural bond to his mother.

"I see her!" Jim screamed! He waved and capered and did everything he could to get the woman's attention on shore, but he was one of many blue soldiers at the rail, and she was past as quickly as he had spotted her.

"Jim, there is no way you spotted your mother on this river! Are you sure?" Henry asked.

"I'm sure!" Jim said, but even now, he began to doubt that he had seen her. "At least I have an idea where to come searching when this war is over."

Jim's elation was contagious, and when word reached Lieutenant Green, he promised Jim that he would write a letter to the military governor in New Orleans and inquire about finding her.

The troops disembarked at the port of New Orleans the next day and waited their turn to board new ships, ones designed to go out into the deep water of the Gulf of Mexico. Lieutenant Green showed the company of about sixty soldiers his map. He pointed out the big blue space of water and how they had come down the long line of the Mississippi and then were heading out to sea. He still would not tell them where they were going, as it was a secret, but he said it must be either west to a Texas port still in Confederate hands or east to Mobile, the last port of the Confederacy east of the Mississippi.

"We'll all know by tomorrow morning," the lieutenant said. "If we wake facing the sun, then to Mobile, it is."

Jim and Henry and the men of Company A were taken to another ship, this one with big paddles on either side of her. She was bigger than the river transport and looked more solidly built. As they descended into the ship's hold, it grew dark and musty, and they joined another hundred men already down there. They packed in as close as they could, with just a tiny space on the floor for them to sit. Their rifles were stored somewhere else, so all they had were their canteens, small haversacks with some food and their packs with their blankets. Most of the men sat on their packs, backs either against the sides of the ships or to each other.

"This must have been what it was like for our people brought over from Africa," Sergeant Nash told the boys, "Except they had it a whole lot worse. They were chained down there, I've been told, and practically starved to death. It's better for us, because we know at the other end of this journey, we will be fighting for our freedom, the freedom of our people."

The fleet pulled away from the docks in New Orleans, and the easy rocking of the river soon gave way to a new feeling. The men could not go out onto the rail like before, and the rocking motion inside the cold ship became more and more severe. At once, almost every man ripped his hat off his head and vomited into his cap. Over and over, the men retched, and the disgusting smell of vomit made any man not already motion sick immediately ill. No one was spared.

The men slowly got used to it, and by rotation, each squad got to come on deck and rinse off at a seawater pump. Jim saw Sergeant Nash walk over and salute a group of white officers on the deck and speak briefly to Lieutenant Green.

When he returned, he gestured away from the setting sun.

"It looks like Mobile for us, boys," he said.

Chapter 20

In the Trenches

Jesse had no time for rest, but he knew he must keep his mind sharp. Rumors began to spread that the fort needed completion fast, as Union troops were on their way and that the Confederate troops assigned to Ft. Blakeley would soon be arriving.

Jesse had four gangs working under his supervision. He had the three groups building Redoubts One, Two and Three. These redoubts anchored the left flank of the Confederate line. However, Jesse's most important decision was to hand-pick his crew for Redoubt Three. His plan — and its success — would depend on it.

He also had to take care of Lucian. Adler was a big help as they shared their meager tent together, but it still pained Jesse every day to see how much his friend suffered. Lucian laughed through his pain, and slowly, the swelling in his face receded.

"I think I'm better-looking now," he had told Jesse and Adler as they pulled him into the tent after his beating. That bravery in the face of pain made Jesse know he had the right men for the job.

"You bet you are!" Adler had said, "No woman will ever look at that mug again without swooning!"

The first part of Jesse's plan was setting the embrasure for the cannon in Redoubt Three. It was tricky and was the most important part of the plan. The trick was that the cannon's opening in the wall must be shifted slightly, one to the left and the other to the right, so that neither of the cannon facing the ravine could quite hit the exact spot where the hidden fork emptied out in front of the works.

Jesse counted on the fact that once the logs were in place, and the final work was done, it would be too much trouble, and there would be too little time remaining, to adjust those firing positions.

By Jesse's calculation, if he could leave just that small gap where the cannon could not fire, it would give the few seconds necessary for the attacking Union force to get close to Redoubt Three, overwhelm the garrison, and break into the fort. Jesse knew that once the main line was breached, the rest of the fort would fall quickly.

The second and most dangerous part of Jesse's plan was his escape. If the Union troops did not know of the gap he had created in the works, then nothing good would come of it. This part of the plan was particularly tricky.

Redoubt One, at the northern end of the Confederate line, butted up against the cliffs overlooking the large impenetrable swamp. It was strongly built, with dugouts built into its walls for the defenders to shelter in case of bombardment. At the bottom of the dugout closest to the end of the line, and hovering just above the cliff, Jesse had discovered his escape route.

The walls of the dugout were lined with logs cut from in front of the earthworks. Jesse's handpicked men had created a false wall at the very bottom of the structure, deep down in the dark recesses of the enclosure and shielded from any penetrating light no matter what time of day. Jesse, Lucian and Adler had dug it at night after most of the workers were back in their camp. When they finally had broken through at the base of the cliff, Jesse now had a way to escape the Confederate lines, find the Union forces and reveal his plan. With Lucian out of the mix, the work had fallen to Jesse and Adler to finish, and they completed it just in time.

Confederate troops began pouring into the works the day after the tunnel was completed.

The Confederate engineer and the big boss accompanied the arriving Rebel officers into the works as they inspected their new entrenchments. Jesse followed, just within earshot, ready to answer any questions or distract the officers from seeing the flaw in his design.

Everything looked good for Jesse's plan at Redoubt One. No one seemed to notice anything out of sorts. This did not surprise Jesse. Redoubt One's tunnel was well-concealed, and Jesse couldn't imagine the officers going down to the bottom of the bombproof and looking at the walls. He felt his tunnel was safe.

Redoubt Two was also well-constructed. It was obvious to the Confederates that Jesse was skilled at building fortifications. This was working just as Jesse had hoped. He had designed Redoubt Two to be exceptionally well-sited in hopes that it would give the Rebels confidence when they got to Redoubt Three, who then might not look so closely.

"Excellent work," the Rebel engineer said to the big boss, who in turn looked at Jesse and nodded approval.

Redoubt Three was next on the inspection tour, and the key to Jesse's plan was the first gun embrasure. He knew that the embrasure was just off by one foot at the site of the gun, but as distance traveled away from the mouth of the cannon, that gap would widen out to a hundred yards wide, plenty of room for the assault to get close.

The Confederate officer dropped into the embrasure and began to inspect the walls. Jesse had placed a trick here that he hoped would distract the officer. He had carved into the top of the earthwork a special "sniper's hide." The front of the work looked just like all other places, but he had dug out a small opening and fitted it with tight cypress logs just the size of a man and at the end had built a small embrasure just wide enough for a rifle to fire through. The construction was small, but the detail and concealment were extraordinarily well-crafted. Just as Jesse had anticipated, this distracted the sharp eye of the artillery officer, and he missed the bigger picture of Jesse's plan.

"Excellent work on this side of the line, men," the engineer said to the big boss. "Extra rations for this crew tonight for a job well done." The boss looked at Jesse, nodded to him again, and he actually smiled at Jesse, that big evil, toothy grin. Success!

The officers moved to the next Redoubt and out of Jesse's section of the line, and he breathed a sigh of relief. His men were done with the construction and would now be taken across the river for the next project.

Now, Jesse just had to figure out a way to get back into the fort when the Union troops arrived.

It was now almost impossible to tell that the black men who had built the forts at Blakeley were former Union soldiers. Months of digging had shredded what was left of their uniforms. Their military bearing, of which they had been so proud, was stripped away from them by the long, relentless days of digging and privation.

Two extra biscuits per man and a big pot of white, lumpy, gravy arrived that evening. As the extra rations were devoured that night, Jesse called his former sergeants together. They had earned the trust of the big boss, and he left them unmolested to do their work. Lucian was well enough to join them.

"Men, the Union Army is on the way. I heard the Rebel officers talking about it. Our job is to make sure when the Blue Coats get here, they understand that we are still Union soldiers. No matter who is in charge when they arrive, we must form up as a regiment," Jesse said. "They must see that we are not slaves, that we wore the blue and served. If something happens to me, I'm counting on you sergeants to form the men. Understood?"

They all nodded in agreement. Several asked if something was going to happen to him. He hated not divulging the plan to them, and he hated to think that he was going to desert them, but he could not tell. They had been lucky Lucian had not told the big boss, and he had to maintain that secrecy.

Chapter 21

A New State

The rocking finally slowed as the ship pulled into a harbor. It was noticeable immediately to the seasick men. Within the hour, the soldiers heard the anchor cables drop. They were allowed up on deck and told to board by squads into small boats that would carry them to shore. It was warmer here, Jim thought, and the trees looked different. They were tall and spindly, with just a plume of long branches hanging down from the top. Palm trees, someone said.

As far as Jim and Henry could see, there was an armada of ships and beetle-like boats filled with blue soldiers scurrying across the water. They could see a small town with regiments forming, staggering and unsteady as they tried to gain their land legs.

Lieutenant Green was waiting for them on the jetty. They disembarked from the boats, opened the crates that carried their rifles and formed up into their company lines.

"You're now in Florida, men," Lieutenant Green told the assembled men. "This is Pensacola. Like Tennessee, this was once Rebel territory. You will be the first colored troops this area has seen, so stay together, be on your best behavior and stick close to camp. We want no trouble, and we will not be here long. When we leave, we will be in enemy territory, so we will camp for a few nights and then get the march underway. Clean yourselves up, and get ready to march and fight, fight and march."

They headed north with thirteen-thousand Union soldiers under General Steele, the sun rising on their right shoulders as they pushed forward each morning. The few locals they passed looked upon them sullenly. No one said anything to the thousands of black soldiers as they marched by. Certainly no one they passed ever imagined that armed black soldiers would even be moving through the deep south.

Lots of talk worked its way up and down the lines. Sergeant Nash told them very little because he didn't know much. Not even Lieutenant Green, their company commander, seemed to know much, so they simply marched and, when not marching, slept on their bedrolls out in the open. They knew one thing: they were moving fast.

One day they came to a small crossroads. As they turned west, Lieutenant Green walked by Sergeant Nash and whispered "We just turned toward Mobile. We are only a few days away from the Rebel lines."

Three days later they marched through deep pine forests and turned south along an old road. Someone said that this was an old Spanish Road, built long before there was even a United States. To the marching men, anything that was remotely interesting broke up the boredom of marching these nondescript dirt roads and the constant pestering of mosquitos.

They smelled the fires before they saw the smoke. Hundreds and hundreds of campfires burned ahead of them, and they could see the glow in the night sky as they came closer to the Union lines. They marched into the early stages of the Union siege, circling the Confederate forts backed up against a river. What the men could see as they moved into their camp was a barren landscape of sandy red dirt, devoid of trees, just their stumps remaining. The red slash of Union and Confederate earthworks facing each other across the fields dominated the landscape.

Jim and Henry watched Lieutenant Green and Sergeant Nash walk over to an officers' meeting. Several of the white officers from the Union regiments already in place pointed out details of the terrain to the incoming troops.

A little while later Sergeant Nash came back to them, called the squad together, and explained what he had been told.

"This is us, boys," Sergeant Nash said as he gestured to the Union lines that ran up against the swamp on their right. "We will be taking this spot in the line, the far-right flank of the Union forces. It is a place of honor. Our works are right across from the Rebel forts they call Redoubts One, Two and Three."

Chapter 22

The Line

Cannon fire boomed nonstop off to the south and left of the Union line. Sergeant Nash's squad, with Jim and Henry, began its part in the siege by being placed in some shallow trenches at the far right of General Steele's line, right up against the bluffs overlooking a giant swamp. Since it was so thick, and since the men could see snakes and alligators down in the swamp from their vantage point, they were not that fearful of an attack. What they were afraid of was a direct hit from one of the Confederate cannons, so they cut timber and spent days building a strong emplacement for themselves.

Sergeant Nash knew that Jim, although he was one of the youngest soldiers, had at least seen and smelled battle. He was a veteran, so he put Jim and Henry in the dugout at the top of the bluff overlooking the swamp. They were the end of the Federal line. Two other men were placed in their rifle pit. Every eight hours, two men were sleeping or cooking while two men were on watch. Every twenty or thirty feet, one of the rifle pits was manned in this way, with a long, thin connecting trench between them. As the soldiers dug the rifle pits deeper and reinforced them with logs, the dirt was piled high in front to increase the protection from snipers.

That was the other big fear the white soldiers they relieved told them about: snipers. The Confederates had a special squad of sharpshooters with rifles that could fire farther than the regular soldier's rifles. They were in the hands of deadly men who were crack shots and whose job it was to pick off, one-by-one, any Union soldiers who exposed themselves above the protection of their works. The deadliest of them all, they said, was a man named

Ingram. It was said he roamed the Rebel lines and had shot men dead at all points on the battlefield.

"Henry," Jim said quietly one evening as they sat in their hole, peering underneath the strong cypress head log that protected them from men like Ingram, "do you get scared out here?"

"Of course I do," Henry replied. "I mostly get lonely for my folks, though. I haven't seen them in months, and they have no idea that I'm so far away from home. I wonder if I will ever see them again."

"I know what you mean," Jim said. "I wonder where my brother Jesse is, and I wonder if I will ever get a chance to find my mother."

"I worry some about dying down here. Or worse, getting wounded like those poor men back in Franklin. I can't imagine anyone down here tending me like Mrs. Richardson did for them back in Franklin. You see the way the white folks look at us down here. And the black folks we have seen down here are so poor, they can barely take care of themselves." Henry referred to the hundreds of freed slaves that had begun following the army as it marched through Florida and lower Alabama. They had a huge camp behind the lines, and they cheered the USCT any time they saw one of its units march past.

"I promise I will look after you if you get hurt down here," Jim said. They both knew they would each try but that the demands of being a soldier might not give either of them that chance.

"What do you aim to do after the war?" Henry asked Jim.

"First, I've got to get back to Louisiana and see if that really was my mother. That's the first thing," Jim said. "Then I aim to get to Nashville and find the Workmans. I've taken quite a shine to their Lucy. I can't seem to stop thinking about her."

Jim's mind wandered to her. His breath caught as he thought about her eyes, gentle and soft, as they looked up at him from the fire. He could almost feel her brush against him as she passed on some errand. Henry startled him from his daydream.

"I wish I could have met her," Henry said. "For me, I might get back to Georgia, but I feel like I want to leave the South and go west. I've heard some of the other boys talking about things being better for us out there. I drove a wagon with a mule team when I was with the Confederate army, and I liked that work. I'm good at it and might be able to make a living as a teamster someday."

Henry had been pulled from his home, a plantation in Georgia where his family members were slaves and driven a mule team with the Rebel army that fought at Franklin.

"That's what I might do," Henry said quietly. He held a finger up to shush Jim. They both listened to a rustle in the swamp, 100 feet below their rifle pit.

They could hear the movement of something down there. It sounded like someone, or something, moving toward them.

A huge roar split the air. Great splashing and fighting and the slap of water.

"Gators," Sergeant Nash said, sidling up beside them. "Those things are ferocious. Either two are fighting each other or one has caught a deer or hog and is killing it right now."

The fight continued, unabated.

"That's probably two big bulls fighting each other. They are territorial, and one of them must have staked a claim below us. I've been throwing our food scraps down there, and I think we have us a pet. That'll keep anyone from sneaking through the swamp and coming up beside or behind us!"

Jim and Henry looked at each other with eyes wide and eyebrows raised. It was comforting to know they had a big alligator on their side, but on the other hand, it was pretty frightening that their neighbor was a big alligator!

The other four men in their position were awake now, and they all peered into the darkness down the slope to try to see the huge alligator fight taking place below them. One of the men, Samson by name, a big man from Arkansas in Sergeant Nash's squad, stood up to get a better view. Morning was coming, and with the dawn, the light was getting better to see.

"I've never seen anything like this," he said. "Back home, we see hogs fight, but they are nothing compared to...

Crack!

Samson was thrown back instantly, dead before he hit the ground, but to everyone's surprise, he did not roll into the trench but toppled over the edge of the cliff. They watched with horror as he rolled down, down and landed right in the middle of the two fighting alligators. The muddy green monsters pounced on him immediately, stopping their fight and together pulling his body underwater. Then, silence. It was over in seconds.

All the men in the hole ducked down and stared at each other in disbelief. Samson was there thirty seconds ago, and now, he was gone. A sharpshooter had killed him, and the gators had taken him away. They were all too afraid to say anything.

"Ingrammmmmmm," they heard a voice call out from the Rebel lines. "Welcome to Alabama!"

Chapter 23

Time to Move

It was time. Jesse had to get through the lines and tell his plan to the Union forces. He knew he held the key to victory for them, but he had to get back to Redoubt No. One.

He sat in a small camp of maybe a hundred workers down by the water's edge. Their job was to go out and repair the works when they got hit by cannon fire from the Union cannon. That was happening almost every day now. Just south of them, another Confederate earthwork at Spanish Fort was getting plastered by the big Union siege guns. The Rebels had ships in the river, in addition to their several forts down there, and they kept up a steady crescendo of explosions against each other.

The big boss strode into the camp at dusk.

"I need a crew to go work on Redoubt No. One," he said, and Jesse volunteered immediately. This was the site of the tunnel he had built, and this offered the perfect chance to get to it.

"I'll go," Jesse said. "I built it; I might as well see how it's holding up."

"Take a dozen men and see what you can do. You'll see the officer in charge up there pretty easy," the big boss said.

It was common enough now for negro work parties to join the Confederate troops in the line. The Rebels did much of the work themselves, but they expected to have the work parties show up and do some of the heavy rebuilding. It was dangerous, but the black men liked working on the north side of the line best because they knew they were across from the Union's colored regiments. They had all been Union soldiers once, and they still were. They all hoped they would be rescued by their brothers in blue.

But Jesse didn't hope. For him, hope was for privates. He was a sergeant major in the Union Army. He made his own hope and made hope for others, too.

Jesse selected his men, making sure not to select Lucian or Adler. He nodded toward them, not knowing if he would ever see his friends again and strode off at the head of his detail.

They arrived to find a cannon ball had ripped a big hole in the top of one of the gun emplacements. Jesse started the men digging around the opening; others worked behind the lines, cutting new logs from their store stacked behind the parapet.

"Sir," Jesse said to the officer in charge of the Confederate garrison, "I built this here redoubt. I'm probably not done building them, either. Do you mind if I look around and see how she is holding up?"

The Rebel officer was an older man, probably in his fifties. He looked too old to be in this exposed position. Jesse also noticed the Confederate soldiers were very young. Many of them looked about Jim's age. The Rebels had been fighting for years, and Jesse could see it in the faces of these men. They looked tough enough to hold the fort, he thought, but these were not the same kind of soldiers he had seen in Forrest's command.

"That's fine," the Rebel officer said. He motioned to one of the young soldiers, leaning on his rifle and watching the men work. "You go with him. If he runs, shoot him."

He said it so casually, it made Jesse's blood run cold. He was not a man to these men, just a thing to get work done. He had spent the last two months building the works to keep them safe, and they did not even acknowledge his sacrifice. On the other hand, Jesse thought it ironic he was actually planning their demise at this very moment.

Jesse started at the south end of the redoubt, the opposite side from his tunnel. He would save the escape for the end, hopefully lulling his guard into being careless. He looked at his guard. Yes, he thought, just about Jim's age. "Where was that boy now?" he wondered. Hopefully he was safe up in Tennessee, maybe in one of the big contraband camps for escaped slaves.

Contraband. That's what the Yankees called the slaves that had run away and followed the Union armies.

He knew they felt safe next to their cannon and regiments of blue-clad soldiers. Maybe Jim had joined a Union colored regiment. He was wearing a blue coat the last time he had seen him walking out of Ft. Henderson.

Jesse studied the walls, descended into dugout after dugout, checking for cave-ins. Most of the time, everyone in each dugout was asleep. They were on watch next, and the Rebels were getting their last bit of sleep before assuming watch. That was good. Maybe his luck would hold.

Usually, his guard would stay outside the dugout. No need to go down into the dugout when the only exit was the opening. That did not change as Jesse came to the last one, the one that housed his tunnel. Jesse descended the ramp and saw three sleeping Rebels rolled in their blankets. It was very dark inside, just one tiny fragment of a candle flickering dimly. Unfortunately, one man was asleep right up against the false door. Jesse had to move him.

He made a quick calculation: locking his eyes on the spot on the hidden log door, he blew out the candle. No one moved. Jesse reached over the man, rolled his sleeping body out of the way, and pulled on the door. It was too dark inside for anyone to notice a black man in the dugout with them. Jesse squeezed into the small opening, pulled the door back in place, and vanished down the tunnel.

As he crawled down the hundred feet of the small shaft, he wondered how long his guard would sit outside the door to the dugout. He hoped he would have a few minutes before the alarm was sounded. He made it to the end of the tunnel and broke away the dirt they had left at the opening to hide it, then stepped out into the swamp.

Chapter 24

Gators!

Each step sucked Jesse's leg down into the muck. He lost his boots immediately. The gas released as he pulled each foot out smelled of death and decay. It was pitch dark as he went into the water, and he did his best to stay close to the cliff wall and solid ground. He hoped it would protect him from shots from above and that it would help him keep his bearings as he worked his way to the Union entrenchments.

He had seen what lived down here. Water moccasins, copperheads and all manner of poisonous snakes and bugs. Clouds of mosquitoes swarmed him, crawling into his eyes, nose and mouth. But the alligators, those are what he feared most. He had seen them on the cliff bank when the sun was out and watched them warm themselves on the bank. At night, they seemed to leave the bank for deeper water. He thought they were night-feeders, and if so, hoped they might be in deeper water away from the cliff. There were no alligators in north Alabama along the Tennessee River where he was from, so he could only guess. He prayed he guessed correctly.

He moved slowly, trying to stay invisible. He rubbed mud all over himself to blend in even more. Ten minutes into his journey, he heard shouts sound above. He was about a hundred yards from the Rebel line, now in no man's land, still close enough to be seen and to be shot. Hopefully, it would be much longer, if ever, before they discovered the tunnel.

He heard the Rebels calling to each other, sounding the alarm. They did it quietly so as not to alert the Union soldiers a thousand yards away. They didn't want to signal to them a spy might be on his way over, in hopes the Yankees might shoot him as he came toward their lines. These Rebels might be young, but they were smart.

Foot by stinking foot, he moved. Branch by branch. The floor of the swamp was lined with cypress knees, small wooden protrusions the size of a man's thumb that stuck up everywhere and made walking even more difficult. They were perfectly designed to trip you if you didn't go slowly.

Two-hundred yards now. The Confederates would have had enough time to send a runner for some of their snipers. That's what they would use to find him. Several of their snipers with the long deadly rifles would be scouring the swamp for him as the sun came up. He had to make it through. He thought about Lucian and Adler and what awaited them when the big boss discovered he was gone. Unfortunately, they would suffer his wrath. It couldn't be helped. They both knew it. Hopefully, they were on their own journey now across the river. They had squirreled away a small raft, and they were to try to float down the river to Mobile and blend in down there, just a couple of displaced slaves. Maybe the big boss would never find them, because if he did, they were dead men.

Three-hundred yards. He could feel his eyes swelling shut from the mosquitoes, and more than once, he thought he felt the movement of a snake out of his path. As long as he didn't step in the nest of a water moccasin, he thought they would leave him alone, but if he did, he knew they would bite. They were protective of their nests.

At five-hundred yards, he felt like he was halfway to the Union lines. By now, he could start to see the sky lightening ever so faintly. That was not good for him. Nothing he saw down here was encouraging, except that it was so thick and overgrown, it might shelter him from eyes above.

At six-hundred yards, he heard the first bellow of the big bull alligators fighting. There were at least two of them, and they sounded like they were right next to him, though he knew they were still farther ahead. They fought and fought and crashed and splashed in the water. Unbelievably, his feet kept propelling him toward the sound. He had to get past them to safety, because he knew that men, the most dangerous of animals, were hunting him from behind.

He got closer and closer, and the battle ahead grew even more fevered. These were two giants clashing. "Please, Lord," he begged they would be exhausted by the time he got to them.

Seven-hundred yards away from the Rebels, and the cliff above was starting to become visible as the dawn approached. He could begin to see the water boiling ahead as the behemoths fought, then….

Crack!

He heard the ball whistle above his head, but far above, and heard the unmistakable sound of it striking home, of a body falling, and he saw a man in blue tumble off the cliff and into the middle of the two alligators. He saw them stop, grab the dead man and slide away. He knew he had seconds before the sniper reloaded, and so the race began.

Chapter 25

Reunion

Rifle balls began to splat against the rifle pit and whistle overhead. Jim grabbed his rifle and crouched behind the head log. The others did the same. He heard a desperate noise below the cliff, the gasping of a man trying to climb.

"Union soldier!" was shouted by the man over and over as he scrambled up the sheer wall, grabbing for any foothold or handhold he could get. He was heading straight for Jim's position.

Smack, smack. The bullets pummeled the head log by Jim's face, and more and more firing erupted from the Confederate lines.

Jim took a chance this was not an attack, that this really was a Union soldier trying to get back to them, so he began to fire back at the Rebels through the slit. The other men did the same. Firing began to erupt all along the line.

Sergeant Nash was next to him now, and he yelled to Jim, "Go help him!"

Jim dropped his rifle, grabbed a shovel from the bottom of the trench and started digging as fast as he could, prizing a small opening against the cliff wall. He hurled dirt backwards, trying to stay as low as possible, and he listened for the sound of the man coming toward them. Closer and closer he came, but his voice was growing tired. Jim knew what a terrible climb that must be for him, alligators below, bullets striking everywhere.

Jim scooped out a small trench that would allow him to pull the man in, and he lay down and extended the shovel down the cliff as far as he could. He could see the man now, or at least a man completely covered in mud from head to toe, desperately trying to get to them.

"Bayonets!" Jim yelled back to the dugout. "Give me your bayonets!"

He pulled his own off his belt and dug it into the earth of the cliff wall.

Zip! A bullet passed just inches from his face.

Several more bayonets landed on his back and beside him, and he rolled low to get his hands on them and began to inch his way down the cliff, building handholds for him and the climbing Union soldier. He was lucky both armies shared the same cliff wall, and it was difficult to get a clean shot from either side once you were over the lip, so Jim descended a few feet down the wall and worked more bayonet hand holds toward the soldier.

He could see the whites of the man's eyes getting closer. He reached his hand down to the man as far as he could, and finally, their fingers touched. Jim reached even farther, and once he had the man's wrist, he pulled with all his might.

Together, they used the bayonet ladder to climb back into the rifle pit. They rolled exhausted onto the floor.

Sergeant Nash trained his rifle on the new arrival.

"Roll away, Jim," Sergeant Nash said, not taking any chances, ready to squeeze his trigger if this was a trick. The other men kept close watch as the Confederate bullets still rained in on them.

The new man lay on his back, chest heaving and unrecognizable in the mud. Eyes closed and exhausted, he continued to gasp, "Union soldier. Union soldier." Jim placed a hand on his shoulder.

"You made it, you made it," Jim said over and over, soothing the exhausted man.

Henry tossed his canteen down to Jim, and Jim poured some in his hand and offered the stranger a drink, then used some of the water to clean his face. He was surprised to see he was a black soldier.

The sun had risen to bathe the landscape in a soft glow, but the bottom of the rifle pit remained in darkness, and Jim continued to wash the mud from the man's face in the dark. The stranger's eyes opened, and he looked around, unfocused. Then his eyes settled on Jim. Jim saw a smile break through the mud. Not just a smile. A grin. Not only a grin but a belly laugh, erupting from the exhausted man.

"Jim?" the man said.

Everyone turned to look at the newcomer. How did he know Jim?

Jim stared at the man, recognizing the voice before the mud was completely washed away. Tears welled in his eyes and his breath caught up short.

As Jim wiped the last of the mud away, his brother's face slowly appeared, just as the morning sunlight bathed the bottom of the hole. Tears streamed down everyone's faces.

The brothers embraced as rifle bullets continued to whip overhead.

Chapter 26

A Respite

Lieutenant Green looked in disbelief at his old sergeant major. In size, he was seemingly half the man he had been at Ft. Henderson; the mud-caked rags hung over his body like those on a scarecrow. Back in Athens, Jesse had seemed to tower over other men, but now, Jesse seemed to be almost the same size as his brother. Jim had grown too, Lieutenant Green noticed. He was becoming a man.

"Welcome home, Sergeant Major," Lieutenant Green said to Jesse.

Jesse rifled in his pocket and pulled out the last fragments of the note Lieutenant Green gave him so long ago.

"Just in case," Jesse said, handing the soggy, illegible paper over. They both laughed.

Jesse recounted his story quickly, nursing a warm cup of coffee Sergeant Nash brought to him. They were all sitting in the company headquarters dugout behind the Union lines, safe from snipers and stray bullets.

"But here is why I made the dash last night, sir," Jesse said. "I oversaw building these three redoubts to your front. I know this position inside and out. I designed a weak spot that you can use to save the lives of many of your men, and it will get you close to Redoubt No. Three undetected. I think it is the key to the whole fort."

"That's astonishing, Jesse," Lieutenant Green said.

Jim watched over their shoulders as his brother drew the plans in the dirt on the floor of the dugout. When he finished, Lieutenant Greene sent an orderly to get a new uniform for Jesse.

"Let's get you out of those rags and up to General Steele. He will want to know this information. The Rebels just evacuated their works at Spanish Fort last night, and the attack is on for Fort Blakeley tonight at five o'clock!"

Jim noticed the shelling had been growing louder from the Union lines into Ft. Blakely all morning. Big cannon boomed all the time, and Jim could tell the intervals were much closer now than ever. His brother had made it just in time.

With Lieutenant Green and Jesse gone to the main headquarters, the instructions for the assault fell to Sergeant Nash to give to the men of the company. They were to prepare to charge the Rebel lines at five o'clock that evening. It was to be a grand charge all along the entire line. All seven thousand USCT troops were ordered to be ready to push forward. The white divisions would also advance at the same time. Sergeant Nash made a point to tell the men they would be part of the main attack this time. He remembered the charge at Nashville, where they had been a diversion, not expected to succeed. This time, they would be in the vanguard.

"Respect. That's what this means for us, men," Sergeant Nash told Jim and Henry and the rest of the company. "They respect us, and we are in the main charge. But we will get through the works first, and we will prove we are one of the best divisions in the United States Army. Understood?"

"Understood!" the men yelled in unison.

By early afternoon, Jesse was back. Sergeant Nash had sent Jim back to the company headquarters, so he could have a few minutes with Jim before the attack. They had not had a second alone since Jesse had miraculously appeared in Jim's trench.

Jim told his story, and Jesse his, as they sipped coffee together. Jesse loved the idea that Jim might have seen their mother on the side of the river in Louisiana.

"That would make sense," Jesse said. "I heard that was where she had been sold. That's a pretty famous plantation down there.

Nottoway. I remember that name. They buy a lot of slaves, or I will say they used to buy a lot of slaves. No more."

The brothers gripped each other's shoulders.

"No more."

They smiled. They both knew they had been part of the greatest event of their generation and perhaps many generations to come. They had earned freedom for their people. They had worn the blue, fought under the Union flag, and tonight, they would make the assault that would break the bonds of slavery forever. This was their fight. They were in it, and at the end, they would go find their mother and start their new life together.

As Jim told Jesse about Lucy, Jesse smiled inside. His little brother had become a man. He enjoyed listening to Jim talk about the future as an equal, not as a shy, quiet, scared boy. He put down his cup, leaned forward and embraced his brother. They held onto each other for a long, long time.

Chapter 27

All or Nothing!

Jesse's plan was coming to fruition faster than he had anticipated. Lieutenant Green's company was to be the spearhead of the attack on the right flank. He was given two other companies, and by four o'clock, the three-hundred men of his command were hidden in the ravine opposite Redoubt No. Three. The other two companies of the 68th USCT had pushed out in front of the lines and had driven in the Confederate pickets. Finally, by April, all the Rebels were manning their trenches, waiting for the assault.

Everyone on both sides knew the war was almost over. General Lee in Virginia was on the run, almost all of the South had been conquered, and just this last pocket of Mobile and its surrounding forts remained. No one knew what life would be like tomorrow. But they all knew that North and South, they would have to do their duty one last day. And they knew not all of them would see tomorrow.

The ravine that sheltered the Union attack in front of Redoubt Three was about thirty yards deep and ran several hundred yards in length. It ended about a hundred yards in front of the big rebel fort as the creek bed turned right to drain into the river, past the Confederate lines. Once past this bend, the 68th would be under Rebel fire from the fort. The most dangerous spot was at the exact point where the Union troops would come out of the ravine. For a few seconds, they would be like the small end of a funnel. Within 10 to 20 yards, they could fan out for their assault. They would take casualties but not the mass destruction they might have had except for Jesse's intervention.

Jesse was given the honor of carrying the American flag. Jim, Sergeant Nash and Henry would be his special honor guard. They would be right at the front with Lieutenant Green. This was the greatest honor any soldier of the regiment could have, but it was also the most dangerous. They lay still among the cypress knees and low grass of the ravine. Jesse had the colors encased in a sheath, and he would remove it just as soon as the order to charge was given. The soldiers lay close, shoulders touching. As they lay on their backs, they could see shells from the Union lines arcing overhead, trailing sparks, as they plunged into the Confederate works.

The Confederates were trying to do their own damage. Mortar shells, fired from big-angled cannon aimed high in the sky, fell all over the Union lines. The safety of the ravine was mitigated by the high arc of these projectiles, and more than once, a mortar round landed in the ravine, shattering Union soldiers and spreading blood and destruction in their wake. The waiting and the randomness of the mortar's impact were the hardest things the men had to endure. Jesse felt Jim grasp his hand and hold it tight as the missiles rained down among them.

"We can do it, Jim," he said to his brother.

"I know we can, Jesse. I know it. If this is my last day on earth, I'm just glad you're with me," Jim said.

"We are back on the Tennessee River with Momma," Jesse said, as much to calm his own nerves as Jim's. "I have that little boat I whittled for you, and we are playing together in the sunlight on the calm bank of the river…"

Boom! A mortar shell landed just up the ravine wall.

"I'm there, Jesse, I'm there with you. Momma's hand is on my shoulder, I see you standing in the water before me, I feel the breeze on my face…"

Boom!! Men screamed.

Lieutenant Green looked at his watch. "One minute, boys!" he yelled, and Jesse and Jim turned to look at each other, holding their gaze for an eternity. Brothers.

Jesse broke away, unsheathed the colors and prepared to be the first across the killing zone. He knew he should be the one to place the colors on the top of the Rebel parapet. He would wave those colors for all to see, a free man, the standard-bearer of his new generation. And Jim would be there. Life was sweet for Jesse at that moment. It made him feel proud he had reached this point in his life, with these men and his brother at his side.

"Charge!" Lieutenant Green shouted, and the men rose as one, bayonets fixed, rifles at the ready. The colors were up, and the men moved forward.

The battle was on!

It was hard for the men to move quickly over the cypress knots (knees?), and more than one man tripped and fell. Jim watched his brother jump and dodge, and like the athlete he was, Jesse got a step ahead of the charging column. The critical junction, Jesse's well-planned spot, was just ahead, ten feet, five feet, and then they were out in the open, the Rebel fort straight in front of them as they turned right.

The cannon fired to destroy them, but it shot harmlessly straight into the side of the ravine, just as Jesse had planned! Jesse glanced at Jim as if to say, "We did it!" and Jim looked into his brother's eyes and saw the triumph, the exhilaration, the pride.

The sniper's bullet hit Jesse in the temple.

He dropped like a stone, dead in a split second. Jim watched in horror as Jesse's hands released the staff of the colors, and Jim dropped his rifle in that same split second. Without missing a step, he scooped up the flag and continued to run forward. As his brother's body slid from view, the red haze of battle and anger boiled up in him. Jim saw the puff of smoke from the Confederate trenches, from the rifle that killed his brother. It was a tiny aperture next to the cannon's mouth, the cannon that had missed killing them all. He didn't know, couldn't know, that only Jesse knew the first man out of the ravine would be the only sure casualty. The great ruse lay in giving that one sniper the perfect shot, and by giving that one man the shot, Jesse would save Jim and dozens more Union soldiers from the cannon's deadly aim.

The Union troops surged from the ravine and sprinted up the slope. As they came out of the low ground, they still had to fight through sharpened log obstacles and rifle fire and as much death and destruction as the Rebels could bring to bear on them, but they rushed forward and blasted their way to the Confederate trenches. Thousands of men in blue, black and white, no longer separated by race but all Union soldiers, ran toward their deaths with one thought: be the first on the parapet!

Jim was beside Lieutenant Green, and Henry was at his other elbow. They all screamed like banshees, throats raw and dust-dry with fear and exhilaration. Bullets buzzed all around, spraying death. Jim was at the base of the fort now, and he thrust the flag's staff into the earth and pulled himself up, up, up toward the top of the parapet.

Henry fired past him, dropping a Rebel trying to shoot Jim. Lieutenant Green fired his pistol into the cannon embrasure as Jim ran up and over the fort's wall, past the sniper's hole, and waved his flag as he reached the top, the first man to reach the Confederate line and wave the American flag!

Bullets whistled by, but he ignored them as he watched more and more Union troops pour over the wall, shooting down the defending garrison and fighting hand to hand. Jim glanced down at his feet, and there, just yards away, he saw the sniper wriggling out of his hole, backing out as fast as he could. Jim knew this was the man who had killed his brother. He raised the flag over his head, its end pointed like a spear, and tensed to hurl it just as the man flipped onto his back. The sniper raised his hands toward Jim, eyes wide and filled with fear, pleading for his life.

Jim drew back his arm, the flag ready to impale the man, this killer, and pinion him to the ground! Anger and sorrow and hate and rage filled him. His arm was ready to fling it down and kill this man, this enemy!

Yet he stopped. All the horror around him, all this death, all the sadness he had seen, melted in him. He saw a man before him, ragged, muddy and scrawny like himself, a man at his mercy, and he could not kill him.

He climbed down the embankment, flag at the ready. Henry descended with him, rifle on the man. The Rebel rose too, eyes pleading for his life, knowing his war was over.

"Surrender?" Jim asked.

The Rebel's shoulders sagged, his head dropped, because he knew it was over.

Jim and Henry stood on the parapet, two slaves turned soldiers, fighters who had won their freedom. Alongside them slouched a Rebel soldier, who just minutes before had been a deadly sniper, now suddenly a prisoner.

They watched the havoc give way to peace, they watched the blood lust go out of all the men around them as the Confederate soldiers surrendered, and the fort fell, and the Rebel flags came down.

The battle was over quickly. Tomorrow would dawn a new day, a day of peace. These soldiers, black and white, would live to see that sunrise.

Chapter 28
Dismissed

The paddle wheel vibration hummed below Jim's feet as the ship slowed at the Nashville docks. Henry by his side at the rail, he watched the shore creep closer and listened to the big gears grind and shift as the paddle came to a stop. The ship coasted to shore. The bow bit the mud, the ramps dropped down, and lines of soldiers formed to disembark back onto Tennessee soil.

Summer was here in Nashville. Without the cool breeze from the momentum of the ship carrying them down the river, sweat broke out on Jim's face. His wool uniform collar and equipment straps trapped the heat and caused him to pull his handkerchief out of his pocket and mop his brow.

The men formed up on the street above, and they stood at rigid attention as Lieutenant Green strode out front to address the men.

"We stand today, one last time, as commander and men of the regiment," he said in his best parade voice. The men glanced at each other, surprised by these words. Jim felt goosebumps prickle his flesh as pride washed over him.

"Today, you will be mustered out of the Union Army, and you will resume your life as civilians. For many of you, this will be your first taste of true freedom. You will not return to bondage. Not now, not ever. Your brothers, men like Jesse Coffee," Lieutenant Green paused as his voice quavered, "have bought this freedom for you. You have earned it by your actions, by the sacrifice of your brothers." Lieutenant Green locked eyes with Jim.

"You can always be proud you fought for the Union and wore the blue, and from now until your dying breath, you will carry in your bosom the right, the earned right, to call yourselves free men.

I will always be your advocate, your friend, and you may write to me whenever you need assistance, and I will do my best to aid you. It is upon you men, the pride of your race, to shape your futures. I commend you for your bravery, your steadfastness under fire, and I wish you Godspeed in your endeavors as citizens of the United States.

"Men, you are dismissed."

It took a moment for the soldiers of the 68th USCT to understand their war was over. As they broke ranks, they flung their caps in the air. They stacked their rifles one last time, clapped each other on the back, hugged their mess mates and sergeants and roared with laughter at the anticipation of Momma's cooking, of long-lost girlfriends, of the sights and sounds of their youth – of going home, home to family and friends.

As the initial excitement ebbed away, however, it was replaced with uncertainty. Jim could see it on the men's faces, as joy turned to bewilderment. "What next?" they all thought. Collectively, this newly released company of men, soldiers just moments before, now realized that many, if not most of them, truly had no place to go.

Lieutenant Green's voice could then be heard over the din.

"Men, I know many of you will be wondering what the future holds for you," he shouted. The men gathered around him. He gestured toward a knot of white men breaking up and moving to small tables behind him.

"The first table will be to receive your pay." The men roared approval!

"The other tables are men from the new Freedmen's Bureau. They will provide you with your passes home, your paperwork for future opportunities and, for some of you, employment right here in Nashville. There is much to do to rebuild all our lives," Lieutenant Green concluded.

The men began to queue at the tables.

Lieutenant Green motioned for Jim to walk with him. Henry followed along.

"Boys, what will you do now?"

Jim was still in a state of shock. He did not answer right away, so Lieutenant Green continued.

"When we buried your brother, Jesse, on the field at Blakeley, I made a promise to myself that I would do my best to look after you. "Henry," he said, turning toward Jim's friend, "I will include you in that statement, too."

"I live up north. It's a long trip up the river, and I will be leaving for my home later today." The lieutenant looked away wistfully, deep in his own thoughts for a moment, thinking of home. "I can't take you with me now, but should you wish to come north, I will help you as I can. For now, the best I can do is to write you both a note that you can use with other white officers here. Many of us will stay behind, and they can know what fine fellows you are."

Lieutenant Green fished in his breast pocket and produced a sheath of letters. He selected two, took out his pen, and wrote the young men's names, one on each piece of paper. He handed them over.

"I knew this day would come soon. The army doesn't want to pay anyone any more than they can get away with, so I wrote these up for some of my favorite soldiers." Lieutenant Green's eyes were moist.

"Losing your brother in that assault was hard for you, Jim. What will you do?"

Jim thought. He could see Jesse fall in his mind all over again. He saw that image all the time. It was a memory he thought would never leave him.

Finally, he said, "I will go to Ft. Negley. I will find Lucy and her parents, and I will cast my lot with them. Someday, I will work my way downriver to find my Momma." He grew quiet again. He remembered her smile, and he thought of the tilt of the woman's head on the shore as they sailed by the plantation in Louisiana.

"I would still be on the banks of the Tennessee River right now but for this war." Jim said. "It has taken a lot from me, no doubt. But I have found a best friend," he gestured to Henry. "I have found a girl I care deeply for, and maybe I have found a family. But mostly, I've grown up, learned to live as a free man, and now I aim to make something of myself. You will receive a letter from me someday, Lieutenant Green, and in that letter, you will hear of all the good things I have accomplished."

Green smiled, clasping Jim's hand in his own. "I have no doubt," he said.

"Well, I'm going to go get in line for that pay you promised!" Henry said, smiling, and with that, Lieutenant Green parted ways with the boys.

Chapter 29

Smokey Row

After the boys received their pay, forty dollars each, a sum they had never thought they would see, they headed through the streets of Nashville. Black men in blue coats, former soldiers of the Union Army, filled the streets.

They knew right where to go. Black regiments had been stationed around Nashville for years now, and the industry of parting soldiers with their money was an industry as old as armies. The areas behind Smokey Row were well-known to many of the men.

Sergeant Nash had seen it before, bars and brothels where soldiers fresh from battle were lured to be separated from their pay. He stood at one of the corners, pleading with his former soldiers to turn left, turn toward the Ft. Negley area where the black families had settled. Most did not.

"Boys, get out of this town as fast as you can," Sergeant Nash, now former sergeant, implored them as the soldiers walked past.

"We are, Sergeant Nash," Henry called to him. "Jim here is crazy to get to Lucy and the Workmans. I'm going with him. But first, we want to get us a fine set of clothes before we see them!"

Jim nodded in agreement.

"Don't stop, boys, keep going. You hold a fortune in your pockets, and these folks know how to separate it from you."

Jim had not thought of this. He had never had anything that anyone wanted. It was a completely foreign experience for him. He had never gone into a store and bought anything before.

The tide of soldiers passed Sergeant Nash, his gestures and pleas in vain as they headed down to Smokey Row and all its wicked pleasures.

The boys moved with the mass of men, carrying them along.

"Let's just see it," Henry pleaded to Jim as they walked. Jim admitted to himself that he was curious about this side of life, and he knew he wanted to get out of his dirty uniform and into a nice set of clothes before he saw Lucy, so he followed Henry up the street.

They saw one of their friends step out of a shop, new suit of brown tweed clothes, shiny leather shoes and a nice bowler hat perched upon his head. He looked for all the world a sophisticated man. Jim and Henry exchanged glances and rushed to the door of the shop.

Piled in the back was a heap of old blue Union coats and pants. A dozen soldiers were inside trying on jackets and pants and hats, and the harried staffers of the clothier fitted everyone as best they could. Jim watched Henry put on a top hat of gigantic proportions, and they laughed at their new-found success!

An hour later and twenty dollars lighter, they stepped out in the street with their new clothes. The oil lights of Smokey Row were just being lit as the boys admired themselves. Jim sported a long frock coat, vest, necktie, trousers and shiny leather shoes. He topped it with a rounded bowler hat. Henry had fallen in love with a top hat and cut a dashing figure in his new dark coat with white trousers. A new watch chain hung from his waistcoat.

Sergeant Nash now stood on a small box at this street corner and continued to implore his fellow soldiers to save some of their money and get out to Ft. Negley at once.

"Leave this sinful place at once, men. Don't you know that a fool and his money are soon parted?!" he cried, but no one listened. These men had been at war for months, and at no point in their lives had they ever had this much freedom. They were determined to have a little fun.

Jim and Henry walked a little farther down the street spying a store window with tins of cheese and meats and freshly baked loaves of bread. They strolled in, elbowed their way to the counter and ordered several items, which they wolfed down ravenously as they walked back out into the streets of Nashville.

With the darkness, Jim noticed a change in the street. For the first time, he began to see the hungry-eyed white men standing at the edges of the crowd of celebrating black men. He had seen those eyes close up more than once but especially almost a year ago, as Forrest's scouts gazed hungrily at Ft. Henderson. The hair on the back of his neck stood up. His senses heightened. Henry, however, did not seem to notice, and when Jim pointed this out, he dismissed it.

"Don't worry, Jim," he said. "there are so many of us, they will not try anything. And besides, you're just getting warmed up here. Soon, you'll be up on the hill, chopping wood for your sweetheart!"

Henry loved to rib Jim about Lucy.

So, on they strolled. They bought some sweet cakes at another store for a dollar each. They had so much money! No worries clouded their judgment. They were two young men in the company of other young men who were experiencing the lure of nightlife for the first time. The sky was the limit for them, and you could see it in their walk and in their devil-may-care attitudes.

The sound of music roared out of a building as they passed by, and the laughter of men and women filled the street with joy. Henry looked at Jim, and before Jim could stop him, Henry dashed inside. Jim followed. He felt they needed to stay together, no matter what.

Jim tasted his first whiskey that night. It went down like fire the first time, but by his third drink, he relaxed. Laughter filled the room, the music made their feet move, and the lights of Smokey Row's bars loosened their inhibitions. Henry laughed; they sang songs with their comrades; Jim felt a joy and reverie he had never experienced.

It wasn't much money they spent on the night and their new clothes, Jim thought. And they had so much money! Lucy would be so happy to see him looking so fine. With his belly full, his face flush, all the joy of the world fell singing in his ears.

Suddenly, the piano stopped, and Sergeant Nash's booming voice echoed around the hall. "Men, don't throw your futures away in here! Save your money and get out to Ft. Negley to the camps! You will need that money to get you started in your new lives!"

A well-dressed white man moved beside Sergeant Nash and put his arm around his shoulders.

"Come now, Sergeant," he said, taking stock of Nash's army uniform. "The boys deserve a night out on the town. Everybody deserves to have some of this fun!" He waved to the crowd with his big cigar and, glancing at the silent piano player, gestured for the music to start again. The crowd erupted back into revelry, and no one saw the two white men rush Sergeant Nash out the back door. Certainly, Jim and Henry did not see it happen.

The rest of the night was a blur to the boys. They staggered arm-in-arm from one establishment to the next. When it ended, neither boy knew. The war was over, they were free men, and the world was theirs.

Chapter 30

Lucy

Jim smelled the vomit before he could open his eyes. He saw his brother fall, bullet to his head, the blood spurting, and he retched again.

So, the puke was his own. And the coolness against his throbbing temple? Mud. Cool mud. He had slept in mud before, so this was nothing new. He lay still as the pain seared his brain, and the memories of his brother's death faded, replaced with a struggling sensation of wondering where he was and what he was doing.

His eyes opened, and he saw Henry. Also, in the mud, in an alley, and people walking past them out in the open street beyond the walls of the buildings. Thankfully, they were in shade, for the light burned his eyes. Seared his eyes. He retched again. He stank.

Henry must be dead, Jim thought. He did not move. Jim knew he, himself, was alive only because he hurt so badly. He hurt everywhere. His mouth was so dry it must be filled with cotton or ashes. The sweet sickening taste of the whiskey from last night lingered on his breath.

Jim had never been hungover; he did not know the ills that whiskey brought, but he had heard stories. The realization of what he was going through embarrassed him.

"I did this to myself?" he thought.

He slid a hand over and punched Henry. He moved, so Henry was not dead, either. He watched Henry go through the same arousal, retching and blinking.

Finally, they both managed to sit up against the side of the building, seats in the cool wet earth. At first, they laughed. They laughed at the fun they had the night before, the singing and the dancing and the great food and the sweet cakes and all that they could remember.

That changed when they reached into their pockets to find their money gone. And their new shoes gone, and their hats gone, and Henry's new watch and chain gone, and even the letters from Lieutenant Green gone. Their new coats were gone. And their new trousers were soaked in mud. They looked at each other, and their laughter dissolved to tears. All they had worked for, gone in an evening.

It was then they noticed they were not alone. A heap of clothes at the dark end of the alley had a hand protruding from it.

Jim and Henry looked at each other with fear. Who was that? Another soldier like themselves? Rolled and now penniless?

Jim crawled over to the man to wake him. He wore a soldier's shirt, but instead of white, it was red with blood. He recognized the Army trousers. Jim pushed the man over onto his back and stared into the broken face of Sergeant Nash. His eyes were wide and lifeless. Jim retched again. He pulled the dead man to him, held his head in his arms and cried.

So much death and so much sadness, and now, Sergeant Nash was gone, too. Henry held them both, his arms wrapping around Jim's shoulders. They sobbed together at their loss, at the waste of another good man gone.

"We're sorry, Sergeant Nash," Jim sobbed to the lifeless eyes. "We should have listened to you. We should have taken you with us, should have been at your side."

Their anguish caught the ears of some passers-by in the street, but they were largely ignored. Smokey Row had seen these situations many times before, and the locals knew to mind their own business.

"Help us," Henry cried. No one stopped.

Finally, two soldiers pulling a cart turned into the alley.

"Get up," one of the men said. "Is your friend dead?" The man was dark and huge. His hooded eyes glowered at the boys, and Jim saw a scar running down his face from eye to chin. He had a cloth wrapped around one arm with letters on it.

"We are with the Provost Guard here in Nashville. Did you boys kill this man?"

"Judas, do those boys look like they could kill anyone?" the other man asked.

He received a slap across his face by the man named Judas for his trouble. "I told you not to call me Judas up here," the big man said.

He pulled a long hardwood staff out of the back of the wagon and used it to prod Sergeant Nash's body. Jim pushed it away and received a quick blow to the head with it. It made the pain even worse, but he shielded Sergeant Nash's body with his own.

"You treat him with respect," Jim said through his tears. "He is a sergeant in the U.S. Army!"

"He ain't nothing now," the big man laughed. "You boys throw him on this cart, and we'll haul him away.

"We will not!" Jim said. We are taking him with us up to Ft. Negley, where we will give him a proper burial."

"The hell you will," the big man said, grim look on his face. "He's worth a few pennies to me to turn his body in, and you'll not rob me of that."

Jim was at him in seconds. All the pain and loss of the last months bubbled up in Jim, and he exploded into the big man. The top of his head found Judas' chin and the big man staggered, teeth cracking at the ferociousness of Jim's assault. The staff dropped from Judas' hand, and Henry had it quickly and waved it in the other man's face.

Jim's fists flew again and again into Judas. His knuckles bled and broke with the violence of the attack, until finally the big man lay still, stunned by the blow to his chin and the flurry of hits to his face and eyes. His nose was clearly broken.

Henry found his voice.

"Get Sergeant Nash on that cart," Henry said to the other man, now cowering against the alley wall.

Jim stood over Judas, hands on his knees, breathing heavy. He straightened.

"Don't you touch him," Jim seethed. "I'll do it." He gently lifted Sergeant Nash's body onto the cart. He arranged his arms across his chest and tidied his bloody collar around his neck. He took the cap off the prostate Judas and laid it gently over Sergeant Nash's face.

"Help me pull, Henry," and the two boys left the alley with Sergeant Nash's body in the cart. They started the long, slow, miserable walk out of Smokey Row and toward the hill crowned by Ft. Negley.

Around lunchtime, they stopped at a stream and did their best to clean themselves up, but first, they attended to Sergeant Nash's body. They undressed him and cleaned him in the water from the stream. Then they scrubbed his clothes and gently redressed him. Sergeant Nash was carefully positioned in the shade. Jim picked some fresh flowers from the creek bank and placed them in his hands across his chest.

They cleaned themselves up. Jim did not want Lucy and the Workmans to see him in such a miserable state.

"What now?" Jim finally asked Henry as they finished cleaning their clothes and began to dress. "Will you go back to Georgia to find your family?"

"Not sure how I will get there," Henry said. "With no money, and without even that paper from Lieutenant Green, I am just like any contraband ex-slave wandering the countryside. I guess I will go down to Franklin and see if the Richardsons can put me to work for some wages. Maybe I can get home that way."

"Once I see Lucy, I will have a better idea for myself. I must see if she remembers me," Jim said. "Then I must get back down to Alabama and make sure someone knows how to find me in case my

Momma makes it back. There is no way for her to know where I am. I keep thinking about her walking back to Alabama from wherever she is, only to get to the cabin by the river and see nothing but graves there."

They napped along the bank until they felt a little better, then began the hike up the hill pulling Sergeant Nash in the cart. The area around Ft. Negley was still covered with the tents and housing of the freedmen. Jim could see in the months they had been gone, an organization to the camp had become evident. As the boys walked down Fourth Avenue, they saw much of the sprawl of shanties around the fort had moved to line the edges of the avenue. Several of the abandoned federal camps had been taken over by the freedmen and their families. Along the streets, modest dwellings more stable than the tents had sprung up.

As they walked past people, men removed their hats and acknowledged their passing. They were not the first people to bring a dead body back from Smokey Row.

They passed the railroad line where so many of his fellow USCT soldiers had died back in the winter at the battle of Nashville. His thoughts again turned to Jesse. That day at Blakeley was never far from his mind.

"The last time I walked this road, I was a soldier," Jim said, mostly to himself. He described the battle to Henry as they walked.

"I came here with nothing," he said, "I return with nothing. But I've learned a lot, Henry. I can do anything I set my mind to. I've learned I will always have my brother's love and that I will always carry him in my heart. I have seen the ocean, the great rivers, the Spanish moss of the swamps of the south. I've seen alligators and the terrible cruelty of men, and I've seen the goodness of men, too."

The Workmans were not hard to find, even though they had moved from the spot Jim remembered. Everyone seemed to know Mr. Workman, who had started a construction business in Nashville since the end of the war. Jim was pointed to a small house down a side street. A gentle breeze kicked up and fluttered sheets on the lines behind the houses; small curtains moved in the windows. It looked like peace.

Jim saw TJ playing in the yard before he saw anyone else. TJ looked taller than he remembered, and Jim reflected on how much he had also grown in the last six months. When TJ saw Jim, he let out a squeal and ran toward him. This brought Mrs. Workman down from the porch.

"I can't believe you're home safe!" Mrs. Workman cried.

She swept him up in a big bear hug, lifting him momentarily off his feet. Jim laughed for the first time all day. He introduced Henry to Mrs. Workman and to Mr. Workman as he came around the corner from the back of the house and put his arm around Jim. He looked in the cart and saw Sergeant Nash.

"Our sergeant," Jim said simply, holding back tears.

Mr. Workman had seen a lot of death, too.

"We'll take him," he said quietly. "We have a very nice cemetery up here. C'mon Henry, help me pull him up the road just a little farther."

Jim started to offer to help when movement at the house caught his attention. Mr. and Mrs. Workman glanced at each other knowingly as Lucy and Jim caught sight of one other.

Jim froze. His arms dropped to his sides as his whole world was filled with her beauty. He did not see Henry and Mr. Workman pull the cart away or notice Mrs. Workman shepherd TJ toward the back of the house. He didn't see Mrs. Workman glance over her shoulder and smile at him as he and Lucy locked eyes.

Like Jim, she had grown up in the last few months. Her eyes shone, and her dress shifted ever so slightly in the gentle breeze. She paused, eyes on Jim's, and she moved gracefully toward him, never taking her gaze from his.

Jim knew in an instant she had not forgotten him. The whole world disappeared except for her radiant face, the beauty she held for him. They reached their hands toward each other, they touched their fingertips, and Jim knew he would never leave her side again.

Epilogue

Frederick Douglas came to Nashville in 1873 to speak at Fisk University. He spoke of hope and the opportunity unfolding in the South during Reconstruction. The nation at that time had Freedmen in Congress, in state governments, in judgeships, and in local governments across the region. The Federal government still held its protective hand across the South with garrisoned troops from Virginia to Texas.

In the crowd the day Douglas spoke, stood a young family. The father, an ex-Union soldier and student at Fisk University, stood with his wife. They held each other tight as the great man spoke words of industriousness, pride, and opportunity. They also held the future. Wrapped tightly against the cool September evening, Lucy held their son.

Jesse Nash Coffee, tiny but lively, with his uncle's eyes, lay swaddled between them.

Notes

The battle of Blakeley took place on the same day that General Lee surrendered the Confederate Army to General Grant at Appomattox, Virginia. Of course, these events happened eight-hundred miles away from each other, and news would not reach Mobile for several days.

The charge of the USCT at Blakeley was one of the largest assaults by African American troops during the Civil War, yet today, it is largely forgotten. The fact that black Union prisoners of war were forced to work on the Confederate lines was also, until recently, clouded from history. Their courage and their contribution to the United States remains undeniable.

As the war ended and the peace began, these men carried the experience of their military life into local, state, and national government. Unfortunately, after Reconstruction, much of their service had to be hidden. As leaders, they became targets in the Jim Crow South. Many paid a heavy price.

Imagine where we would be today if their leadership had been allowed to thrive. Their legacy lives on, however, and I am convinced our future remains brighter with their stories told.

To my readers, thank you.

I hope you will share this book.

I would love to hear from you. My email is

kvetters@gmail.com.

References

Towns, Peggy Allen, *Duty Driven.* ISBN 978-1-4772-5556-8. 2012

Andrews, Christopher Columbus, History of the Campaign of Mobile. ISBN 9781429016476. 1889

Logsden, David R. *Eyewitness at the Battle of Nashville.* ISBN 0-9626018-6-1. 2004

Jacobson, Eric. *For Cause and For Country. A Study of the Affair at Spring Hill and the Battle of Franklin.* ISBN 978-1-940669-09-0. 2013

Groom, Winston. *Shrouds of Glory: From Atlanta to Nashville.* ISBN 0-8021-4061-0. 1995

Brueske, Paul. The Last Siege. The Mobile Campaign, Alabama 1865. ISBN 978-1-61200-631-4

Knight, James R. *Hood's Tennessee Campaign, The Desperate Venture of a Desperate Man.* ISBN 978-1-62585-130-7. 2014

Lovett, Bobby L. The African-American History of Nashville, TN 1780-1930. ISBN 1-55728-555-1. 1999

https://www.battleofnashvilletrust.org/
https://fortnegleypark.org/
https://boft.org/

Freedom Spring Study Guide

By Kurt Vetters

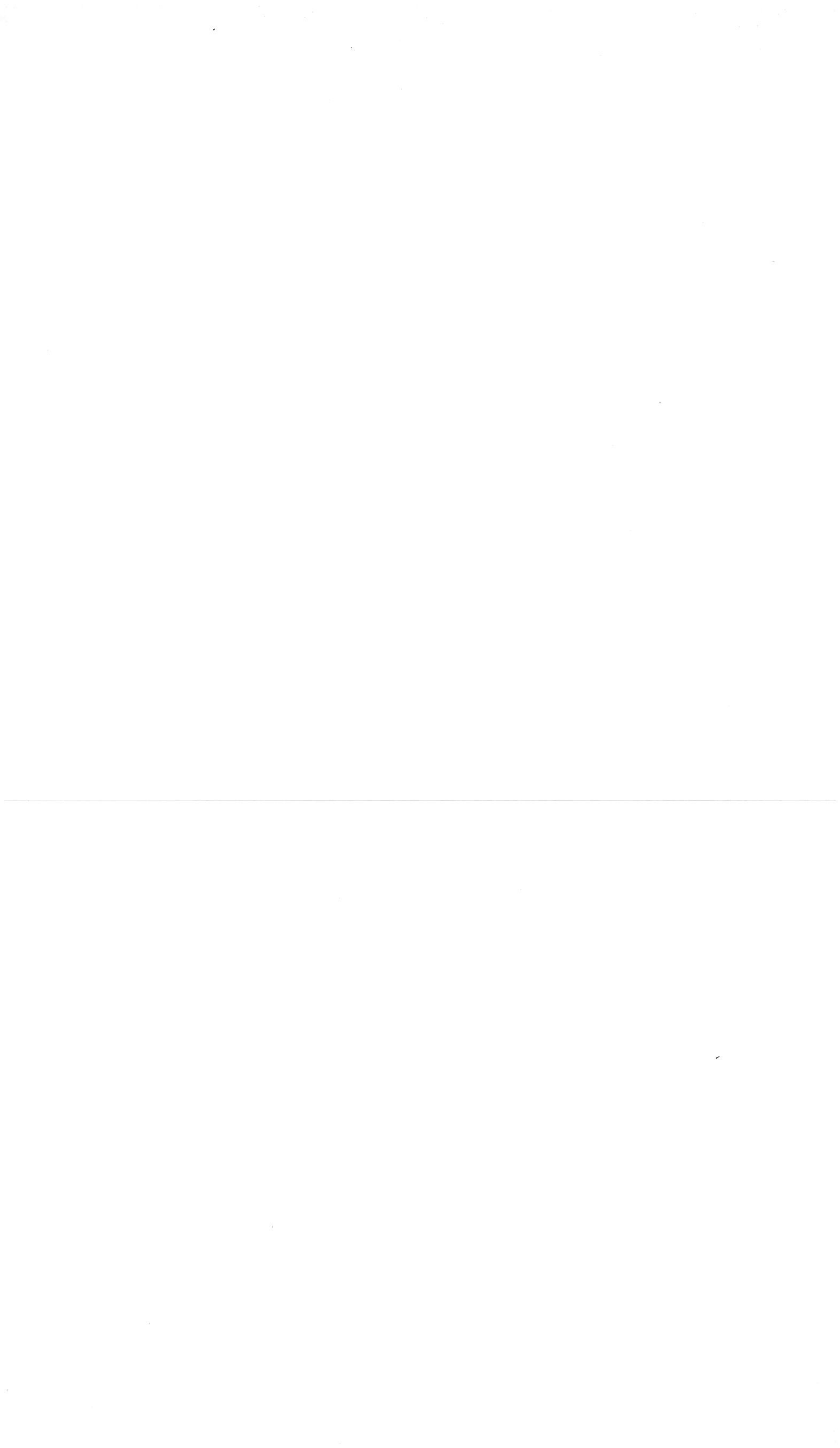

Book Summary:

Freedom Spring tells the story of a young slave who finds his path to freedom in the United States Army fighting to free his people and forge a path for himself in the new world.

1. Brother-brother Relationship

Q. Discuss Jim's relationship with his brother Jesse and how this relationship changes.
A. Jim feels his brother has abandoned him to a life of slavery and resents his escape from bondage. Jesse has always been a father-figure for Jim, and he looks up to him, but the feeling of abandonment is reinforced at the fort. This forces Jim to become his own man without his brother's help.

Jim also must deal with the complications of his isolation the last year at Marse Robert's cabin. He is forced to trust others in his journeys and decide who is trustworthy and who is not. Jim is forced to build his own self-confidence.

Jim must face the harsh realities of his father, his brother, and his friends by the end of the book and he learns that he can succeed in life.

2. Understanding the Civil War and it's causes

Q. Jim only sees how the war and his escape from slavery affect him at the beginning of the book. By the end of the story, how does Jim see the world now that he has seen so much of it up close?
A. Jim's journeys take him across the country and put him in contact with people different from himself, such as Lieutenant Green and Colonel Campbell. They represent the differing attitudes of the Union soldiers toward the freed slaves. He also

meets his fellow African American soldiers in Sergeant Nash and Henry, as well as Judas. Probably most importantly for Jim's future, he meets Lucy and her family, and they show him the path toward the future.

3. Slavery

Q. How do Jim's thoughts about slavery change over the course of the book?
A. Initially Jim only knows bondage. His view of the world places him in frightening situations at every turn, situations he sees as beyond his control. As he progresses through his time in the Union army, he begins to see that he has control of his own destiny in the choices he makes. By the end, he can see a future full of hope.

Prologue

Chapter Summary: Jim's master dies, and Jim leaves the cabin for his walk to freedom.
Discussion Starters: Have you ever felt as alone as Jim felt? How did you cope?
Activity Suggestions: Jim and Jesse's work is making earthworks to channel water. Build a channel to direct the water of the next rain.

Chapter 1: Time to Go

Chapter Summary: Jim starts his journey east to Fort Henderson where he hopes his brother and the Union army will be.
Discussion Starters: Do you have any secret signals between you and your friends?
Activity Suggestions: Look up Pope's Tavern in Florence Alabama. It is still there and is a museum. Better yet, go see it!

Chapter 2: Found!

Chapter Summary: Jim finds the fort, his brother, and some Rebel spies, but he is not believed.
Discussion Starters: Have you ever not been believed?
Activity Suggestions: Use a telescope or binoculars to see something far away.

Chapter 3: The Fort

Chapter Summary: Jesse shows Jim around the fort and Jim learns his father was Marse, which caused his mother to be sold down river. Activity is spotted in town.
Discussion Starters: Do you think Jesse was fair to tell Jim about his father in the manner he did?
Activity Suggestions: Research Civil War earthworks.

Chapter 4: Rebs!

Chapter Summary: The Rebel army begins to surround Fort Henderson.
Discussion Starters: Have you ever felt different by putting on a piece of clothing?
Activity Suggestions: Find a piece of clothing or jewelry that makes you feel stronger.

Chapter 5: An Attack

Chapter Summary: The Rebel cannon open fire on the fort all night, and Jim takes the place of the Colonel's orderly.
Discussion Starters: Can you imagine being under a cannon bombardment?
Activity Suggestions: Search the internet for Civil War Cannon firing. Learn how gun-powder-filled shells work.

Chapter 6: A Truce

Chapter Summary: Jim leads the Colonel's horse around the rebel lines.
Discussion Starters: Did you spot the trick that the Rebels were playing on the Colonel and his aide?
Activity Suggestions: Look for a *Where's Waldo* book in your library. Can you spot differences in a crowd?

Chapter 7: The Ruse

Chapter Summary: The Fort is surrendered, and Jim leaves with the white officers.
Discussion Starters: Have you ever felt defeated, perhaps after your favorite team loses an important game?
Activity Suggestions: Look up and listen to the bugle calls of Taps and Retreat. See the difference?

Chapter 8: Change of Circumstance

Chapter Summary: Jesse watches Rebel General Forrest take charge of the fort and turn the soldiers back into slaves.
Discussion Starters: How must it feel from the Union soldiers to go from soldiers to slaves again so quickly?
Activity Suggestions: Look at pictures from the Civil war and try to decide what that person's job was? Not everyone was a fighter.

Chapter 9: The Retreat

Chapter Summary: Jim retreats with the Union army into Tennessee.
Discussion Starters: Have you ever thought what life was like before cars, when people walked long distances?
Activity Suggestions: Look at a map to see where the action is taking place.

Chapter 10: A Long Walk

Chapter Summary: Jesse walks through Alabama south and then meets the new boss.
Discussion Starters: Can you tell what city Elyton Alabama grew into?
Activity Suggestions: Research the term "Home Guards." Could you do this job?

Chapter 11: Spies

Chapter Summary: Jim goes fishing and saves a Rebel's life.
Discussion Starters: Discuss the decisions Jim is having to make for the first time.
Activity Suggestions: Round-Robin response: what were Jim's options? Did he do the right thing?

Chapter 12: The Pact

Chapter Summary: Jesse plans to make he and his men soldiers again.
Discussion Starters: Talk about the decisions Jesse is making to regain his dignity.
Activity Suggestions: Draw a map of the fort from the information given. Look up Fort Blakeley.

Chapter 13: Nashville

Chapter Summary: Jim arrives at Ft Negley and meets the Workman family. Lucy gets his attention.
Discussion Starters: Was Jim right in not turning in the wounded Rebel scout?
Activity Suggestions: Spend a few minutes talking to your neighbor about the differences at that time of Jim talking to Mattie and Jim talking to Lucy.

Chapter 14: Fort Negley

Chapter Summary: The Rebel army is on the move and heading to Nashville while Jim stands guard at Fort Negley and gets to know the Workmans and falls in love with Lucy.
Discussion Starters: Contrast the slave workers with Jesse at Fort Blakeley versus the freed workers at Fort Negley.
Activity Suggestions: Find pictures of Fort Negley and talk about how different it looked than Fort Henderson.

Chapter 15: Trust

Chapter Summary: Jesse earns the trust of the Big Boss, and secretly puts his plan into action.
Discussion Starters: Jesse uses his brains, not his brawn, to earn the trust of the Big Boss. Discuss.
Activity Suggestions: Research the Cant Hook, invented in 1857. Many times, ideas originate in several places around the same time.

Chapter 16: Assault!

Chapter Summary: First day of the Battle of Nashville.
Discussion Starters: Discuss what the term "feint" means.
Activity Suggestions: Find a map of the battle of Nashville on the first day and see the ground the men charged over. Look for General Steedman's assault.

Chapter 17: A Good Plan

Chapter Summary: Jesse outlines his plan to weaken Fort Blakeley.
Discussion Starters: Do you understand Jesse's plan to compromise the Rebel fort?
Activity Suggestions: Play one of your favorite games and try to think of what your opponent will do next, before they make their move.

Chapter 18: New Friend

Chapter Summary: Jim meets Henry at the Richardson's, and Henry joins him in Sergeant Nash's regiment.
Discussion Starters: Did you know both sides took care of each other's wounded soldiers?
Activity Suggestions: Compare the Union army and the Confederate armies at this time of the war. Which one seems stronger and why?

Chapter 19: An Exciting Journey

Chapter Summary: The regiment sails down to New Orleans and out into the Gulf of Mexico, preparing to attack Mobile, last bastion of the Confederacy.
Discussion Starters: Has anyone been out to sea, and has anyone been seasick?
Activity Suggestions: Can you find town on the Mississippi River called White House? What would slaves have worked on there?

Chapter 20: In the Trenches

Chapter Summary: Jesse's plan is almost ready and escapes the attention of the Rebel officers.
Discussion Starters: Building forts must have been hard work. What's the hardest work you have ever done?
Activity Suggestions: Quickly write how you think Jesse's plan will unfold once the Union troops arrive outside the fort.

Chapter 21: A New State

Chapter Summary: Jim lands in Florida and marches to Fort Blakeley. Unbeknownst to him, his regiment is right across from the forts his brother has built.
Discussion Starters: How would the people of Florida and Alabama react to Black Union troops who had only seen Blacks as slaves?
Activity Suggestions: Draw a map for your friends and see if they can follow it to a place of your choosing.

Chapter 22: The Line

Chapter Summary: Jim and Henry talk about their future, and a comrade is killed by the deadly sniper Ingram.
Discussion Starters: What was happening elsewhere in the Civil War during April 1864?
Activity Suggestions: Read about Sharpshooter Charles Ingram of Missouri. His rifle is still on display.

Chapter23: Time to Move

Chapter Summary: Jesse escapes the fort!
Discussion Starters: How did Jesse calculate his escape from the Confederates and from the alligators?
Activity Suggestions: How far is 100 feet? Can you measure it to see how far Jesse slid down to the swamp?

Chapter 24: Gators!

Chapter Summary: Jesse inches through the dangerous swamp to the Union lines.
Discussion Starters: Jesse has great courage. Who do you know today who has exhibited great courage?
Activity Suggestions: This is a good time to research swamps of south Alabama and the alligators and snakes which inhabit them.

Chapter 25: Reunion

Chapter Summary: Jesse reaches the Union lines and finds his brother Jim.
Discussion Starters: Have you ever had a reunion with a loved one after a long time apart?
Activity Suggestions: Write about a reunion you have experienced and share it with another student. Listen to theirs too.
Activity Suggestions: Research the Reconstruction era after the Civil War.

Chapter 26: A Respite

Chapter Summary: Jesse and Jim get a few minutes to talk before the big charge.
Discussion Starters: Do you have a younger sibling? Think about how your relationship would be in this situation.
Activity Suggestions: Research how many Union troops were of African American descent in the Civil War.

Chapter 27: All or Nothing!

Chapter Summary: The charge!
Discussion Starters: When Jim faces the sniper, does he do the right thing?
Activity Suggestions: Can you find pictures of the Fort Blakeley charge?

Chapter 28: Dismissed

Chapter Summary: The soldiers are mustered out of the army.
Discussion Starters: How much money were USCT soldiers paid monthly during the Civil War?
Activity Suggestions: Discuss some changes the boys will experience being on their own now.

Chapter 29: Smokey Row

Chapter Summary: The boys live it up in Nashville on Smokey Row.
Discussion Starters: Are you surprised or disappointed that the boys turned toward Smokey Row?
Activity Suggestions: Can you think of ways in your life that you have been enticed to spend your money on the wrong things? Discuss in a round-robin group.

Chapter 30: Lucy

Chapter Summary: Jim returns home.
Discussion Starters: Has Freedom Spring taught you anything new about the American Civil War?
Activity Suggestions: For a novel of the Confederate experience during these trying times, read Confederate Winter by Kurt Vetters.

Kurt M. Vetters

A former US Army Cavalry Captain and Civil War reenactor, Kurt Vetters' passion is telling the stories of the regular soldiers who lived, fought and died in the greatest cataclysm the United States has ever seen.

He served as Executive Officer of Delta Company, 1st Battalion 40th Armor and was awarded two Army Commendation Medals. He is currently the Vice President of a medical supply company and serves on several boards of directors. He is a former American Legion Post Commander.

A military history enthusiast, he has written for the Greenfield Indiana Daily Reporter with an emphasis on Veteran's Issues.

He is from Sheffield, Alabama, grew up in Birmingham, lived for many years in Indiana, and now resides in Florence, Alabama.

Also by Kurt M. Vetters

Confederate Winter

Confederate Winter is historical fiction based on a true family story.

The author's great, great, great grandfather, William Sweeney, fought as a Confederate soldier at the tender age of 14. His father, John, had been drafted the year before into the Union Army. ***Confederate Winter*** is their story.

By 1864 the Confederacy is on the verge of defeat. Atlanta has fallen and Confederate General John Bell Hood's army is in retreat. But Hood formulates a bold plan to re-capture Nashville, the great base for the Union army in the West. A victory could change the course of the war. Hood needs manpower, however, and sends his conscription parties out to scour the countryside.

Confederate Winter tells the story of a true-life family caught up in this grand adventure. The Federals conscript John Sweeney, the father, in late 1863 as General Sherman prepares his march on Atlanta and the sea. His son William is left in charge of the family farm, until one early fall morning…

★★★★★ *A moving glimpse of humanity during desperate and devastating times*

"Kurt Vetters' highly entertaining and easily read story provides a fascinating portrayal of the emotional and physical tragedies of the Civil War as seen through the eyes of a young boy trying to do the right thing, as well as a fascinating historical account of the era's military strategy and tactics. Highly recommended."

- Jim Steele, Author

Made in the USA
Middletown, DE
30 April 2022

65009143R00094